Mated to the Myth

Mated to the Myth

Highland Shifters Book 8

Caroline S. Hilliard

Copyright © 2023 by Cathrine T. Sletta (aka Caroline S. Hilliard)

All rights reserved.

This publication is the sole property of the author, and may not be reproduced, as a whole or in portions, without the express written permission of the author. This publication may not be stored in a retrieval system or uploaded for distribution to others. Thank you for respecting the amount of work that has gone into creating this book.

Produced in Norway.

This book is a work of fiction and the product of the author's imagination. Names, characters, organizations, locations, and events are either the product of the author's imagination or used fictitiously. Any resemblance to actual persons, living or dead, organizations, events or locations is purely coincidental.

ISBN: 979-8-8613-0259-3

Copy edited by Lia Fairchild

Cover design by Munch + Nano
Thank you for creating such a beautiful cover for my story.

CONTENTS

About this book	i
Chapter 1	1
Chapter 2	7
Chapter 3	12
Chapter 4	19
Chapter 5	23
Chapter 6	29
Chapter 7	34
Chapter 8	39
Chapter 9	46
Chapter 10	53
Chapter 11	58
Chapter 12	63
Chapter 13	72
Chapter 14	78
Chapter 15	85
Chapter 16	91
Chapter 17	96
Chapter 18	101
Chapter 19	107
Chapter 20	113

Chapter 21	121
Chapter 22	126
Chapter 23	132
Chapter 24	137
Chapter 25	142
Chapter 26	149
Chapter 27	155
Chapter 28	162
Chapter 29	166
Chapter 30	174
Chapter 31	180
Chapter 32	187
Chapter 33	195
Chapter 34	202
Chapter 35	206
Chapter 36	209
Chapter 37	214
Chapter 38	222
Chapter 39	226
Chapter 40	233
Chapter 41	239
Chapter 42	245
Chapter 43	251

him that immediately drew her gaze, but she had made sure not to give him more than a cursory glance now and then. He was gorgeous with his white-blond hair and his high cheekbones, not to mention his beautiful blue eyes.

But it wasn't only his looks that had grabbed her attention. It was the strong yet calming power surrounding him like a safe haven in the middle of a sea of turmoil. And it had made her want to throw her arms around him and hold him tightly to let his power soothe away all her doubts and fears.

Squeezing her eyes shut, she swallowed hard. Gawen was too good for someone like her with an inability to trust and commit to a man. And even if she hadn't felt that way, he was still a shifter and would eventually want a mate, a concept that filled her with dread just thinking about it.

For as long as she could remember, she had felt her mother's sadness and resentment for being forced to mate her father. And unlike Henry, it had instilled in her a healthy skepticism toward shifter men and their mating instincts. She had promised herself never to date a shifter, and she had no plans to break that promise. Not even for a man like Gawen.

I'm such a fucking idiot! Nes curled her fingers into fists. She should never have let Henry talk her into going with them. He had been worried about her safety after Amber had shown up at her restaurant, and Nes had given in to his wishes, appreciating his concern for her. She had missed him, as the only one in her family she felt she owed anything.

But subjecting herself to being around Gawen was a mistake. She wasn't worried that he would act like anything other than a gentleman toward her, but she feared what being in his presence would do to her and her resolve to stay away from him. He was a temptation she didn't want or need.

If only her overactive mind would acknowledge that and allow her to stuff the image of Gawen's glowing eyes and straining muscles into the back of her mind. She must be giving off a constant scent of arousal with what that scene was doing to her lady parts, but thankfully, that didn't seem to be a problem with so many newly mated couples around. Mates were more attuned to the arousal of their mates than anyone else, so her scent probably wouldn't even register with any of them unless it became overpowering. But she wasn't going to allow it to go that far.

Pulling in a deep breath before letting it out slowly, Nes willed herself to relax and think of something else. Her restaurant was the first thing that came to mind.

She had left it in the capable hands of Olivia, her assistant manager and head server, so there was no reason to worry about business going ahead as usual. It was one of the reasons she had trained Olivia as her assistant in the first place. But this was the first time the woman would be solely in charge for more than a day at a time. And although Nes had no doubt Olivia was up for the task, it had still felt strange to leave so abruptly without knowing exactly when she would return.

However, there was something else that worried Nes more than her restaurant. The possibility of a reunion with her mother, Louisa. Nes hadn't been back to visit the pack or her parents since she left several years ago, and she had no wish to do so anytime soon. But with her mother leaving the pack and Henry getting back in touch with her, there was a chance they would decide to meet up.

Most people would probably say Louisa wasn't to blame for what had happened to her, but Nes wasn't sure she agreed. Her mother hadn't been very forthcoming with the details of what had really happened when she was coerced into mating Nes's father, but ultimately it had been Louisa's own decision to let the mating take place a few weeks after she was delivered to the pack against her will.

Her mother could have kept refusing her father, and eventually he would have given up, but the fact was that she hadn't. So in Nes's opinion, her mother was at least partially to blame for the resulting mating disaster. And Nes would never forgive either of her parents for her broken childhood.

Nes's life had improved significantly when she left all of them behind and moved to London, and then later to Wick. She might be irreparably broken from a shifter's perspective, but she could make her own choices and live the life she wanted. Even though she might never have a significant other to share it with.

CHAPTER 3

Gawen

Gawen stepped out of the vehicle and followed Trevor and Jennie into Leith's house. The others were yet to arrive, but Trevor had the code to the door, granting them access.

"I think I'll go for a swim. It helps me clear my head and think." Gawen felt bad for wanting to escape and not helping prepare an early lunch for everyone, but there wasn't all that much they could do until Michael, Steph, Duncan, and Julianne arrived with the groceries.

Trevor chuckled and turned to meet Gawen's gaze. "You sound like Leith. He has an affinity for water as well—unsurprisingly."

Gawen smiled. "Yes, that's to be expected. I won't be long."

He hurried down the stairs with his bag. After reaching the bottom level of the house, he quickly changed into his shorts before leaving through the downstairs entrance.

Loch Ness was glinting in the sunlight, like it was trying to entice him into its embrace. But he didn't need the encouragement. Water was his element, and no matter how badly life was treating him, delving into its depths always lightened his mood and quieted the voices in his head. It was almost like it washed away not only the dirt on his skin but also the grime clogging his mind.

Gawen breathed out a deep sigh of relief as soon as he stepped into the water. If he didn't owe it to everyone to help catch and destroy Amber, he would have happily left everything behind to stay beneath the waves for days. But he couldn't, not yet. He would as soon as the evil woman was taken care of, though. It might help him combat his growing feelings for Henry's sister.

Diving deep, he pushed his thoughts of the beautiful female wolf to the back of his mind, filling it instead with the sensations of the cold water caressing his skin.

Amber. He had to keep his focus on the vile creature who had held him hostage for who knew how long. He had no recollection of who had originally captured him or what had happened to him during the time he was held against his will, but he knew he had been a prisoner for almost two years before he woke up in the clearing where Fia and Amber were facing off.

But who had initially taken him and done something to his mind to keep him confused and unaware of what was going on? Was it Amber, or had she just happened to find him at some point and decided to keep him? He had tried time and again during the last few days to force himself to remember, but no matter how hard he tried, there was nothing. It was like his mind had been completely wiped clean for the duration of his imprisonment.

Gawen shuddered at the thought of what might have been done to him in that time, and he wasn't sure if he should regret not knowing or count himself lucky for not remembering anything. There had to have been a reason he was taken, but whether it was to keep him away from someone or do something to him was impossible to know. He had no recollections that would suggest one over the other.

He let himself float slowly to the surface before opening his eyes and staring up at the blue summer sky of Scotland. This was his country, and a beautiful country it was with its numerous lochs and green mountains and glens. It was where he belonged, and yet he didn't feel like he fit in with the people inhabiting this land. He was too different.

Perhaps he needed to do what he had been told since he was a child—toughen up. Shut down the feelings that always made him seem weak in the eyes of others and become more ruthless and arrogant. He was powerful, more powerful than most other shifters, but it went against his conscience to use his power for anything other than helping others. Using it for personal gain felt wrong, unless the gain was to see someone healthy and happy.

Gawen silently dove beneath the surface again and swam languidly toward the small beach close to Leith's house. He had an innate sense of where he was when he was in the water, so he didn't need his eyes to help him find his way.

As soon as he was sufficiently close to the shore, he set his feet down and rose out of the water, only to be met by a shriek. His eyes snapped open and landed on Nes standing less than two feet in front of him and staring at him with wide eyes and her mouth hanging open. She was standing with water reaching up to caress the underside of her breasts, and he couldn't help how his gaze dipped to linger on her hard nipples poking at the scanty blue material covering her full breasts.

Groaning, he dragged his gaze back up to her face. His cock was already hardening in his shorts, and he was thankful that it wasn't clearly visible through the water.

"Were you trying to scare me, or are you going to claim that you were somehow lost down there?" Crossing her arms under her chest, Nes scowled at him.

He was helpless to prevent his gaze from lowering to her breasts again, even more prominent now with her arms pushing them up, before he squeezed his eyes shut. "I'm sorry, Nes. I never meant to scare you." His voice was rough with need, and he winced at what she must think of him.

"Well, you didn't scare me exactly, but you did give me a fright."

Opening his eyes, he took in her narrowed eyes. Before he could repeat his apology, she continued.

"Were you sneaking up on me on purpose?" Her gaze raked down his torso before staring down into the water directly at his groin.

She couldn't see his lower half through the gently moving surface, but his cock twitched all the same. Gawen cleared his throat before he answered. "No, I didn't think to look since I didn't expect anyone to be in the water. At least I didn't crash right into you. I could've hurt you. I'll be more careful next time."

Nodding slowly, Nes let her arms sink into the water before taking a step toward him.

Gawen frowned, wondering what she was doing. He had expected her to walk away, not take a step closer. And she was still looking down into the water instead of meeting his gaze.

Perhaps he should have anticipated it with where she was staring, but he wasn't prepared when she reached out and palmed his erection. His whole body froze, and he held his breath, not sure whether to rejoice in her willingness to touch him or worry about what she had planned.

She hadn't shown any sign that she found him attractive or that she wanted to get to know him, so he didn't know how to interpret her current behavior.

Her hand slid up his shaft until she reached the head of his cock before curling her fingers over the waistband of his shorts and brushing them gently against his sensitive tip.

Gawen hunched forward a little, bunching his abs to try to stay still while she touched him. Having Nes's full attention was more than he had dared to hope for, and the last thing he wanted to do was to cause her to pull away.

Was this a sign that she liked him, or was she just fascinated by the fact that he was different? He'd had women approach him before just to satisfy their curiosity about him but with no real interest in him as a person other than to brag to their friends that they had fucked the outcast. It had been humiliating to be used like that, but he had allowed it anyway, since he had craved the physical contact.

Nes let out a small moan as her fingertips traced the rim of his cockhead, making him shudder with how good it felt. "You're so big. Would you even—" Her voice choked off, and she snatched her hand away. Her head snapped up and she stared at him with a look of horror on her face.

He couldn't help the small whine that escaped him at the loss of her touch, but he managed to stay still, even though he wanted to reach for her and pull her into his arms just to feel her close.

She backed away from him a couple of steps, never breaking their eye contact. Then she closed her eyes and visibly swallowed. "I'm so sorry, Gawen. That was... I don't know what's wrong with me."

Gawen took in her beautiful features and her short spiky black hair before he spoke in a soft voice. "There's nothing wrong with you. You're perfect."

Her eyes flew open. "No. No, don't say that. Don't try to gloss over how I just treated you. Taking liberties like that isn't okay."

Her flustered words made him smile. She might be curious about him, but at least she didn't seem to have a premeditated agenda to give him a test run without caring about his feelings. "Then let's call it even. I subjected you to a horror show last night, and you touched me a little more intimately than you intended just now. I don't want this to make things awkward between us."

Her brows drew together in a frown, and she nodded slowly. "Thank you, Gawen. You're being too generous. Are you coming back to the house?"

"Not yet. I'll be there soon, though." When he no longer had a throbbing steel bar in his shorts. Hopefully, it would soften quickly once Nes left, and he could focus on something other than her wet body and soft touch.

"Okay." She nodded. "See you soon then."

CHAPTER 4

Nes

Nes managed to keep her devastation from showing on her face until she turned away. Wading back toward the beach, she let the awfulness of what she had done sink in, and her shoulders sagged with shame and embarrassment.

What on earth had driven her to touch him like that? She had never been particularly forward with men, and all of a sudden she was groping a virtual stranger without a second thought.

If she didn't know better, she would have claimed she was acting on instinct, because it was the only way to explain her behavior in a way that didn't classify it as harassment. But it wasn't instinct, just simple fascination, and that was a good thing, since she didn't want a mate, and meeting her true mate would make that impossible to avoid.

After reaching the beach, she grabbed her towel

and wrapped it around her before starting up the path toward the house. The urge to turn her head and check if Gawen was still standing where she had left him was there, but she resisted it.

There was no doubt he had been turned on, but that didn't mean he had any interest in her other than pure lust brought on by the situation. She didn't know what he was, but shifters were sexual creatures by nature, and she wouldn't be surprised if other supernaturals were the same.

Nes frowned when she recalled his words. *There's nothing wrong with you. You're perfect.* She had taken that to mean he forgave her for her transgression, but was that really what he had meant? Or had he actually paid her a compliment?

Heat spread through her body at the thought. She wouldn't allow anything to develop between them no matter what he felt or wanted, but she couldn't deny that it would feel good to have someone like Gawen desire her.

Nes was well aware she didn't fit the typical image of a shifter female, with her tomboy looks and her less-than-adequate flirting skills. But then she had never wanted to attract a possible mate, and her looks had served her well in that respect.

After entering the house, she took a couple of steps toward the stairs before she stopped. There was a window next to the entrance overlooking the loch and the beach. A quick peek to check if she could see Gawen wouldn't hurt, and it would let her know if he was still down there or already on his way toward the house.

Her heart sped up when she approached the

window, and she couldn't help feeling like she was spying on him. But the sight that met her was disappointing. The gorgeous man was nowhere to be seen no matter how carefully she scanned the surface of the water.

Sighing in frustration, she turned away from the window. *Serves me right for lusting after a man I don't really want. I don't want a mate. Not even him.* Pressing her lips together in annoyance, she hurried up the stairs to the living room.

She gathered her clothes from the chair where she had left them and entered the bathroom to change. The others would have lunch ready soon, so it was time to join them.

The reason she had gone down for a swim in the first place was to grab a few minutes alone after the long ride in the back seat of Leith's car in the company of Henry and his mate. Her brother had spent most of the time trying to get her to tell him about her life since she left the pack, and she had spent most of the time trying to evade his endless questions.

It had been exhausting, and by the time they had reached Leith's house, she had been ready to explode. Even the prospect of seeing Gawen again after their awkward conversation on the phone hadn't concerned her in her eagerness to escape her brother.

But she had still counted herself lucky when she had reached the beach without having encountered the tall blond god on her way. That was, of course, until he suddenly shot up out of the water right in front of her and almost gave her a heart attack.

Licking her dry lips, she looked down at her fingers. Just minutes ago she had caressed the silky skin of his cock, wishing she could let her eyes feast on his hard length like the night before. If he had pulled her into his arms right then and kissed her, she probably would have let him. Or maybe not. It was more likely that him making a move toward her would have snapped her out of whatever trance she was in.

She sighed deeply and lifted her head to stare at herself in the mirror. There she was, the woman who had easily dismissed the three shifter males who had shown her any attention so far in her life, making her think that steering clear of mating would be a breeze. But that was before meeting a gorgeous man with beautiful blue eyes and a beautiful personality to match. Unless she took control of her attraction to him and kept her distance, he might well end up being her downfall.

CHAPTER 5

Gawen

Gawen was the last one to show up for lunch, and he entered the kitchen just as everyone was finding their seats at the dining table.

There were a lot of them gathered around Leith and Sabrina's long table. Including their hosts, they were seventeen people, and most of them were true-mated couples. It was nothing short of extraordinary to have so many true mates gathered in one place at the same time.

Trevor, Jennie, Leith, and Sabrina were seated at the opposite end of the table from Gawen. Then there were Bryson and Fia, Duncan and Julianne, Michael and Steph, Callum and Vamika, and Henry and Eleanor. Nes was seated between Henry and Vamika, her eyes on her plate.

The only other single male at the table apart from himself was Aidan, an exceptionally powerful supernatural calling himself an elemental enforcer due to his power being tied to the earth. Gawen wasn't entirely sure how that worked, but perhaps he would get a chance to witness Aidan's formidable power the next time they met Amber. Because that was why Aidan had agreed to help them. Amber had proven to be both destructive and lethal, and if not contained, she might in time become a threat to more than just the shifter population she was currently focusing on.

Callum cleared his throat, drawing everyone's attention to him. The blond wolf had a frown on his face as he glanced around the table at the people looking expectantly back at him. "As you all know we have been trying to locate Amber since we left Wick this morning."

He glanced at the beautiful black-haired woman sitting by his side, giving her a small smile before his expression reverted to its previous frown. "And although we have some new information, we can't tell you where Amber is at the moment or where she's heading. As expected, she picked up her daughter, Mary, in Glasgow early this morning, but since then her trail has gone cold. Her car is still in Glasgow. We've had someone verify it's hers to be sure. But we don't think Amber and her daughter are still there. Most likely they have acquired some other kind of transportation and left the city, but we haven't been able to discover where or how. At least not yet."

"Have you checked footage from available cameras in the area?" Duncan put an arm protectively around Julianne's shoulders.

Callum nodded. "As much as we've had time for, yes. And although there are more cameras around than people are aware of, there aren't nearly enough to trace someone's movements accurately, not even in the main cities in Scotland. We won't give up, but with the time it takes to track her, we always seem to be at least one step behind, and it makes it difficult to predict her next move."

Henry narrowed his eyes. "Which means we need to approach this the way we talked about at dinner last night. We have to make Amber come to us by presenting her with an opportunity she can't resist." His gaze landed on Gawen. "And I think I might know how to do that. Gawen, can you come with me for a second?"

Gawen's spine stiffened in apprehension before he nodded. He had a feeling he wasn't going to like whatever it was Henry was about to ask him. But he already knew he would say yes to whatever it was.

After rising from the table, Gawen followed Henry out into the hallway and down the stairs to the living room. He trusted his new alpha, but he couldn't help the way his heart sped up as his mind tried to anticipate what was coming.

As soon as they reached the living room, Henry turned to Gawen with a small smile on his face. But Gawen wasn't fooled into believing that whatever Henry was about to ask him to do would be easy. Thankfully, Henry didn't leave him to wonder for long.

"I have a proposition for you that I suspect will draw Amber's attention. It will give her the opportunity to achieve the two things she wants the most, gain power and kill shifters."

Henry paused and put his hand on Gawen's

shoulder, staring into his eyes. "However, it will put her focus on you with the intention to kill you. And although we will all be there to protect you and destroy her when she comes for you, I don't want you to agree to do this if you don't want to. I would do it myself if I could, but that's no longer possible."

Gawen frowned. "What exactly would you like me to do?"

Henry stared at him for a couple of seconds before he spoke. "I want you to pretend you love my sister and the two of you are about to be mated."

Every ounce of air in Gawen's lungs left his body in a whoosh, like he had just received a hard punch to the stomach. Nes. Beautiful Nes. Images of her and what he wanted to do to her if she was his filled his mind, and he struggled to pull air back into his lungs. Pretending to love her would be easy, but it wouldn't be pretending for long. Having her close and looking at him like she actually cared would be heaven—and hell when he crashed back into reality.

"I'm sorry I asked." Henry pulled his hand away from Gawen's shoulder and took a step back. "I can see that you're struggling with the idea. Don't worry about it. We'll come up with another way to get Amber's attention."

"No." Gawen forced the word out with the little breath he had before pulling in a lungful of air. "I'll do it. But only if Nes is okay with it. Any sign that it makes her uncomfortable, and I can't agree to make her pretend with me."

Henry gave a sharp nod. "Agreed. Thank you, Gawen. I'll talk to Nes."

"I want to be there when you do." Gawen stared

into Henry's eyes, letting his alpha see his determination. "I want to see her reaction firsthand, so even if she agrees I know where we stand."

Henry cocked his head. "Are you sure? It might be better if I talk to her alone. You don't know her like I do."

"I'm sure." Crossing his arms over his chest, he stiffened his spine. "I need to know how this affects her, or I can't agree to do it."

"Okay." Henry nodded. "Stay here while I go get her." He didn't wait for a reply before he stepped around Gawen and hurried up the stairs.

Heart racing, Gawen stared straight ahead without seeing what was in front of him. What if she was disgusted by the idea—disgusted by the mere notion of pretending to be his? He dreaded seeing that look on her face more than anything else. But at least it would be an honest reaction, and he would know where he stood. And if he was lucky, it would be enough to kill his budding feelings for her.

Gawen shook his head slowly. As painful as that might be, the real danger to his heart was if she agreed and convincingly acted the part of being in love with him. Even knowing it was fake, he knew it would affect him. He would have to work hard to keep his own feelings from developing, but he feared he would end up with his heart broken.

Footsteps sounded on the stairs behind him. "What are you up to now, brother? Why do I get the feeling you are ready to feed me to the witch?"

Gawen chewed on the inside of his cheek. To the wolf hybrid would be more accurate, but he would leave it to Henry to explain that.

Nes passed him before she turned and raised an eyebrow at him. "Are you here to help Henry convince me to do whatever it is he wants me to do? Or does he have some sinister plan for you as well? My brother is all about the greater good, so I guess I shouldn't be surprised he's ready to offer me up as a sacrifice."

"Oh, stop the melodrama." Henry chuckled. "I won't let any harm come to you, or to Gawen for that matter."

"Ah, so you're going to be a sacrifice as well then." A small smile pulled at the corner of her lips as she nodded to him, and Gawen couldn't help noticing how soft her lips looked. Would he get to kiss her as part of the performance they were going to be putting on? He hoped so. That might make his eventual heartbreak worth it.

"No one is getting sacrificed." Henry chuckled again. "But I want you to work together."

"How?" Nes's eyes narrowed as she stared at her brother.

Henry's expression sobered. "I want you two to pretend you have fallen in love and you're going to mate."

Gawen's breathing ceased as he waited for Nes's reaction. A part of him was telling himself to look away so he didn't have to witness the look of horror that was bound to appear on her face, but it was like his gaze was fused to her face, unable to look away for even a second.

Her eyes widened, and her lips parted before her gaze met his, but no sound passed her lips for several seconds. She didn't look disgusted, though, which was something.

CHAPTER 6

Nes

Nes was struggling to process what her brother had just said. She blinked a couple of times while staring into Gawen's eyes.

He was staring right back at her, his body completely still and his expression blank.

If only she had gotten some kind of indication of what he was thinking. She had no idea whether he hated the idea or was fine with it. But since Henry had spoken to Gawen first, he must have already said yes or there wouldn't have been any reason for Henry to present the idea to her as well.

Pulling in a shaky breath, she tore her gaze away from the blond man and let it drop to her feet. "I'll do my best to play the part, but only if Gawen feels comfortable with this arrangement."

Henry snorted. "That's pretty much exactly what he said about you, so it sounds to me like you're both up for the challenge. Are you ready to kiss and prove it?"

"What?" Her voice was a high-pitched squeak, and her head snapped up to stare wide-eyed at her brother's wicked grin. Nes could feel heat rising into her face, and her heart was beating like a jackhammer in her chest. She had already imagined kissing the gorgeous man several times since she met him the day before, but being practically ordered to do it by her brother was not how she had pictured it happening.

"Henry, there's no need for that. Stop embarrassing your sister."

Gawen's angry voice hit her like a slap, and she winced. *Great, he hates the idea of kissing me. Just my luck to sign up to be his pretend girlfriend, and he doesn't want any physical contact.* Except, he hadn't seemed to hate her touch in the water earlier. His cock had been hard as steel, and he hadn't pulled away from her. But whether it meant anything other than that he was a virile man and she was a woman in a bikini, she had no idea.

Henry's grin slipped. "I'm sorry, but I'm only half joking. You have to be willing to show some affection, or Amber is going to see through the act immediately. It's important to make her believe your love is real, or she'll understand it's a trap."

"We will get to that." Gawen's voice was back to its usual warm tone. "But you have to give us some time to discuss how we're going to approach this."

Nes could feel Gawen's eyes on her. The embarrassment at her reaction to Henry telling them to kiss was eating at her, but she forced herself to meet Gawen's gaze. Her inexperience with real romantic relationships must be evident by now, but since this wasn't going to be anything like a real relationship, it shouldn't matter.

She nodded. "Yes, we need to make a plan." Her voice was shaky, but she ignored it. "We need to make sure it's believable without crossing any boundaries we're not willing to cross."

Gawen's lips curved into a smile as he studied her face. "Let's go get some lunch, and we can bring it down here to talk about it while we eat. I didn't even get one bite before Henry had his bright idea."

"I guess I was a little impatient to find out if it was something you would agree to." Henry smiled at Gawen before swinging his gaze to Nes. "Thank you both for accepting this so readily. Now we just have to find a way to alert Amber of your intended mating without making her suspicious."

Henry headed back up the stairs, and Gawen followed, leaving her to bring up the rear. Had there been a glint of mischief in her brother's eyes? She hadn't really paid attention while her mind was spinning with the fact that she was going to spend the next couple of days, or perhaps longer, close to Gawen. It shattered her earlier vow to herself to stay away from him, but she couldn't seem to care at the moment. Her body was filled with an anticipation so strong it was making her jittery with excitement, which was all kinds of wrong, since all Gawen had agreed to was giving a convincing performance.

They filed into the kitchen where everyone was busy eating and talking, but the room soon grew quiet when Henry cleared his throat.

"I think we have a way to attract Amber's attention and entice her to come to us." Henry smiled at the people seated around the table before turning his head to look at Gawen and Nes. "Gawen and my sister have agreed to pretend to be in love and about to be mated. Most of us already know Gawen is powerful, and Amber is sure to know that as well. If we can find a way to communicate what is about to happen, I doubt she'll be able to resist taking advantage of the situation."

Nes felt her face grow hot again. Everyone's attention was on her and Gawen, and it made her uncomfortable. She always tried to act like nothing bothered her, but the truth was she didn't like to be the center of attention. The only place she didn't mind having people's eyes on her was at her restaurant, but acting as a host at work wasn't the same as being stared at for more personal reasons.

Trevor nodded. "Clever. As long as we're prepared when Amber arrives, this might be our best shot. But I can't help wondering why she didn't try mating you to someone before, Gawen?"

"I think at least one of the intended mates has to be a willing participant." Sabrina's eyes were narrow in thought. "Forcing two people to mate might be beyond Amber's mind-control abilities."

"That's a possibility." Steph nodded. "And with someone like Gawen with strong magic of his own, Amber might've realized how risky it would be to try. Keeping someone subdued and confused is one thing, but making them carry out tasks that require more conscious awareness is completely different as well as another level of fucked up. Fortunately, I think Sabrina is right, and Amber doesn't have the power to do that. She has to rely on at least one willing party."

"We should go to Fearolc." Duncan turned to look

at Trevor. "The house is more than big enough for all of us, and the garden is expansive enough for an outdoor celebration. It will give Amber the opportunity to watch us without too many innocent bystanders getting in the way and being at risk. The population is mostly shifter, and some of them might even agree to help us."

"Sounds like a plan." Trevor swung his gaze around the table where people were nodding their agreement. "And you already have some surveillance measures set up for my property, don't you, Callum?"

The blond wolf smiled. "I do, and more can be arranged. Needless to say, it's much easier to keep track of a person within a small area rather than trying to follow them all over the place. We'll make sure to have the whole property covered and then some." He smiled down at his mate sitting by his side. "My assistant and I will take care of it."

Vamika laughed. "Oh, so I'm your assistant now? Well, I'm sure I'll be able to *assist* you with all kinds of things, boss."

Callum's smile widened, and he winked at his mate. "I'm counting on it."

"In that case I think we'll leave the planning to you." Gawen turned to Nes with a smile lighting up his face, but she managed to keep her expression neutral. "Nes and I will be downstairs planning our act. Just come get us when you're ready to leave."

CHAPTER 7

Nes

Nes dutifully grabbed her plate, which was already filled with the food she had chosen earlier, before following Gawen back down the stairs to the living room. She wasn't so sure she would be able to eat anything, though, with the way her stomach was fluttering with an equal measure of dread and excitement. Just the prospect of being alone with the man was enough to make her whole body jittery, and that was before even considering what they had to do together to come across as a couple in love.

Gawen sat down close to the end of the large couch, leaving her to pause and debate whether to sit close to him or toward the other end. For her own sanity, she should put some distance between them, but for the sake of what they were trying to achieve, she needed to get used to being close to the man.

"I'm not going to kiss you without warning even if

you choose to sit next to me, Nes." Gawen had a small smile on his face when she met his gaze.

Her face heated when she realized he had been reading the indecision on her face and probably the reason behind it as well. It was embarrassing how much like a teenager she was acting around this man, and she needed to stop it if she was going to be able to act the part of his woman.

After pulling in a deep breath and relaxing her features into a small smile, she sat down next to him, leaving only a couple of inches between their thighs. Too bad he wasn't going to kiss her without warning. It would be so much easier if he just took charge and did what he would have done if he actually cared about her. Even if it might leave her reeling with shock, at least she would be spared the constant evaluations of what to do next.

"How do you really feel about this?" Gawen's voice was soft without giving away what he was thinking. "I know you agreed, but you almost seem scared of me now. If you regret your decision, I'm sure your brother will understand."

Nes bit her bottom lip for a second. He was right. She felt anxious around him but probably not for the reason he thought. There might be a way to curb some of her fear, though.

Without letting her doubts get in the way, she turned her head and closed the distance between them before pressing her lips to his for a brief kiss.

She didn't meet his gaze when she pulled away. Instead, she picked up her knife and fork and focused on her food.

A burst of laughter sounded from beside her.

"What was that?"

Nes stopped with her fork halfway to her mouth. "Our first kiss. I just wanted to get it out of the way. I don't like first kisses. They're awkward."

"I hate to break it to you, little bird, but that wasn't a kiss."

She almost choked on the food she had just shoved into her mouth. And she kept her eyes on her plate until she finished chewing and swallowing. What the fuck was he talking about? She had just put her lips on his, and by her definition that constituted a kiss. Did he have a different definition?

Slowly, she turned her head to look at him and was startled to find his gaze lingering on her with a considering expression on his face. "Would you allow me to show you?"

Her heart did a somersault in her chest, and she had to take a slow breath before she could answer. "Okay." Her voice came out more even than she had dared to hope for.

He stared into her eyes for a second before lifting his hand and trailing his fingers across her cheek and into her hair. Then he leaned in slowly, too slowly judging by the way her lungs seized in her chest.

His lips brushed against hers gently, and for a second she thought that was all he was going to do. But she was wrong.

The next thing she knew, Gawen's lips pressed against hers, his hand in her hair tightening to hold her firmly in place while his mouth moved against hers. His tongue flicked out, tasting her lips, and she parted them on a shaky sigh.

He didn't ignore her invitation, but swiped his

tongue inside her mouth, brushing over her own tongue and eliciting a moan from her. Then, he gripped her hair so tightly it stung her scalp, and he dived in for the kill.

His tongue dominated her mouth in a way she had never experienced before, taking possession while she did her best to keep up. This wasn't just a kiss, but a show of passion that was lighting up her insides with burning desire. If it didn't stop soon, she would need a change of panties and perhaps a little time alone.

"Well, I can see that my uncertainty about you being able to be convincing was groundless."

Nes jerked and pulled her head back so fast, Gawen didn't have time to loosen his grip on her hair before she yanked it from his fist. "Fuck." She put her hand up to massage her burning scalp as she turned to scowl at her brother. "What do you want? You were the one who asked us to do this, so why don't you leave us to work on our performance?" The pain fueled her anger as well as her irritation at being interrupted in the middle of the best kiss she had ever had.

Henry lifted his hands, showing her his palms in a placating gesture. "I'm sorry. I didn't mean to interrupt." He didn't look sorry, though. An amused smirk covered his face as he looked between her and Gawen. "I just came to tell you we'll be leaving in half an hour, so you should probably spend a few minutes consuming your food in between devouring each other's lips."

After rolling her eyes at him, she looked down at her plate. She had an appetite, but food wasn't what she craved at the moment. A kiss alone shouldn't be able to heat her body like that. It never had before, so why now with a man she was only going to spend a few days with at the most? It was unfair really. But perhaps that meant there were humans out there who could affect her like Gawen just had. The thought didn't make her happy, though. On the contrary, it was enough to douse the lingering heat in her body and leave her cold.

"I'm sorry."

Gawen's words broke through her thoughts as her brother made his way up the stairs. She turned to look at him with a frown. "What for?"

His eyes searched hers like he was looking for a sign that she understood what he was apologizing for before he spoke. "For almost pulling your hair out. I wasn't aware I had such a tight grip on you."

"Oh. That's okay." *You can pull my hair as much as you want as long as you kiss me like that.* But instead of telling him that, she just gave him a smile.

Gawen's gaze lingered on her for another couple of seconds like he wanted to say something more, but in the end he sighed and turned to stare down at his food. "I guess we should eat."

His less than enthusiastic tone made her smile widen. He didn't sound like he relished the idea of eating, and she hoped that meant he would rather have continued with what they were doing before they were interrupted.

CHAPTER 8

Gawen

Gawen forced himself to chew and swallow, but it might as well have been cardboard he was eating instead of a salad with bacon, chicken, and feta cheese. His body was humming with desire, and all he wanted to do was pull Nes close for another scorching hot kiss. Because *holy fuck*. He'd had no doubt that kissing her would be fantastic, but he hadn't expected it to blow his mind. Who knew how it would have ended if his alpha hadn't interfered.

But at least he would get to kiss her again. If they were going to be convincing as a couple on the verge of mating, they would have to be all over each other every chance they got. And he couldn't wait.

His only concern was how long he would be able to keep up the pretense that this was just a show they were putting on. His dick was hard as a result of their kiss, and he didn't think he would be able to keep that from happening the next time. It was easily explained as a natural reaction, but he was still scared it would intimidate her into pulling away from him.

Or perhaps she wouldn't. Nes had surprised him by stepping closer and gently fondling him in the water earlier. But did that mean she was attracted to him or was it just a result of curiosity? And which would be better? She was still his alpha's sister, and although Henry was the one who had asked them to act like lovers, he might feel differently if they hit it off for real.

"If you'll excuse me, I need a few minutes before we leave." Nes grabbed her plate and hurried toward the stairs, looking like she couldn't wait to get out of his presence.

"I think we should ride in the same car." He watched as her shoulders tensed, and she stopped just before putting her foot on the first step to go upstairs. "We have no idea where Amber is at the moment, so we have to assume she's watching us at all times."

She visibly swallowed before she turned to look at him with what appeared to be a fake smile on her face. "Sure. No problem." Then she practically ran up the stairs.

Frowning, Gawen pushed his plate away. He couldn't stomach another bite as he considered Nes's hurried retreat. Had she changed her mind about doing this with him? Perhaps he had scared her with the intensity of the kiss. But she had responded, and he hadn't been able to hold back when her tongue slid against his and her hands fisted his shirt, holding him close.

And there you go again, thinking that someone like her can fall for someone like you. You're being an idiot as usual, mistaking lust for love.

Sinking back against the couch cushions, he squeezed his eyes shut. "No, not now. I won't let you fill my mind with negativity." He realized he was whispering in response to voices in his own mind, and it was probably a sign of insanity or something, but he didn't care. Sometimes it worked better to speak the words instead of just thinking them to make the voices shut up.

Without waiting for more of his insecurities to voice their opinion, he opened his eyes and got up. Taking his plate with him, he hurried up the stairs to join the others and prepare to leave.

∞∞∞

Gawen sighed with relief when Nes got into the back seat of Trevor's car beside him. He hadn't been sure she actually would, not after the way she had resisted meeting his gaze when he joined the rest of them in the kitchen after she left him in the living room.

But here she was ready to sit beside him during the time it would take them to get to Fearolc and Trevor's estate. Gawen hadn't been to that particular area of Scotland before, but he had been to the west coast, and he looked forward to seeing the lush green scenery again. And with the beautiful woman next to him by his side, he had a feeling he would be enjoying it even more than he had the last time, even though the scenery could never compete with her beauty.

"I look forward to showing you my estate." There was a smile in Trevor's voice. "I had originally planned to spend a relaxing few weeks there before going back to America where I live most of the time, but then I met this beautiful woman"—he smiled at Jennie, who was sitting in the passenger seat—"and before I knew it, all hell broke loose."

Jennie laughed. "You make it sound like this mess is all my fault. Would you rather not have met me?" Her voice was teasing.

"Hell no." He chuckled. "But I wouldn't have minded a honeymoon that was a little more relaxing."

"Yes, I guess this has all been a bit much for a man your age. Perhaps we should consider getting a live-in nurse to help with your daily care." Jennie's voice was filled with barely contained laughter.

Trevor glanced at her with one eyebrow raised in surprise. "You really want another female to live in our house and tend to my needs?"

His blond mate shook her head slowly. "I never said anything about a *female* nurse."

The alpha wolf's laughter boomed through the car. "Like I would ever allow that to happen." He grabbed Jennie's hand and lifted it to kiss her knuckles. "Nice try, though. I have a feeling life will never get boring with you around. I can't believe I once dreaded taking a mate. But that was, of course, before I found my true mate."

Gawen smiled. He wished he would be that lucky. It sounded more like a fairy tale than real life, though, and he wasn't fool enough to believe it would happen to him.

Glancing over at Nes, he noticed she was staring out of the side window, her jaw tense like she was finding this whole situation uncomfortable. Before he could stop himself, he reached over and took her hand in his.

Her body stiffened, and she turned her head to stare at him, but she didn't pull her hand away.

"Relax." He smiled at her. "We're pretending, remember?"

Her chest expanded when she pulled in a deep breath. "Yes." The word flowed out with her exhale, and the tension in her body seemed to dissipate with it. A small smile crept over her lips. "I'm sorry. This is just so…unusual, and I haven't really had time to get used to the idea yet."

Gawen nodded. "I know." He squeezed her hand gently. "And that's why we need to work on it." With his eyes on hers, he lifted her hand to his lips and kissed her knuckles just like Trevor had done with his mate a minute ago. It was the perfect gesture to show affection without too much intimacy, and he would have to come up with more ways to do that. It would help them keep this believable without it getting awkward between them.

Her gaze dropped to his mouth for a second before she turned to look straight ahead, her head falling back to rest against the headrest.

Frowning, he studied her face. Why hadn't he noticed it before? There were dark circles under her eyes, and her eyelids were drooping slightly. He had assumed she had gotten a good night's sleep the night before, unlike himself, but that didn't look like it was the case. "You look tired. Why don't you lie down and get some rest?"

The corner of her mouth ticked up as she turned to look at him. "You don't mind? I thought you wanted us to practice being a couple."

Gawen chuckled. "I do, and we are. Putting your head in my lap is a perfect way of showing everyone we're a couple."

Trevor burst out laughing. "I couldn't agree with you more, Gawen."

Nes's eyes widened, her face turning a beautiful shade of red. "That's—"

"Going a bit far, I know." He squeezed her hand. "I'm sorry. It was just too good an opportunity to miss. You can slap me if you want. I deserve it."

Narrowing her eyes at him, she shook her head slowly. "No, I think I can come up with a better way to get you back."

Laughter sounded from the front of the car again, this time from both Trevor and Jennie.

"You already sound like a couple." Jennie turned to look at them over her shoulder. "I don't think you're going to have any trouble pulling this off."

"Let's hope not." Gawen winked at Nes and patted his thigh. "What do you think?"

She pursed her lips and studied his face before removing her seat belt. "Fine."

He watched her as she moved around before curling up on the seat with her back toward the front. But it wasn't until she put her head in his lap that he realized his mistake. The way she was lying put her mouth less than an inch from his crotch, and he had no doubt she knew exactly the effect that had on him.

His cock immediately took notice and started thickening, and it didn't take him long to understand that his predicament was worse than he had first thought. His rapidly filling shaft was trapped between his balls and his thigh, and it was already getting uncomfortable.

He tipped his pelvis a little forward to check if it would be enough to free his cock, but it did nothing to alleviate the situation.

Nes winked up at him, no doubt enjoying what she was doing to him. But he didn't think she realized the extent of his discomfort.

"Thank you for letting me lie down." She smiled up at him sweetly, but there was a wicked glint in her eyes. She raised her hand to her mouth before sliding her middle finger slowly into her mouth, her lips fitting snugly around her digit.

Gawen's eyes just about bugged out of his head at the sight, and he pressed his lips together not to make a sound. *Fuck.* He could well imagine how she would look with her lips wrapped around his cock, and how amazing it would feel, and he didn't need those thoughts in his head right now.

But it was too late. His dick swelled, and the pain made him wince. He had to do something to free his cock even at the risk of coming off as a deviant for fondling himself while people could see him.

After sliding one hand under Nes's head, he lifted it a little before widening his legs and using his other hand to free his trapped erection. The relief was immediate, and he sighed with contentment as he lowered her head back down to rest in his lap.

Sorry. He mouthed the word in response to her startled expression. There was no hiding his hard cock with how it strained against the fabric of his pants, but then she was partly to blame for his condition, and she knew it.

CHAPTER 9

Nes

Nes bit her bottom lip not to burst out laughing. At first she had thought she had gone too far with her teasing when Gawen had decided to move her head off his lap, but that was before she understood the real reason for the slight panic in his eyes.

Her actions had had the desired effect on him, except for the fact that his cock had been stuck, causing him some unintentional discomfort.

But she had neglected to take into account his impressive size and how close her mouth actually was to the bulge in his pants. She wouldn't even have to move an inch to be able to kiss the thick ridge, and that thought alone was enough to light a fire in her lower belly.

Giving blowjobs wasn't something she had been a particular fan of, most likely because the human men she had been with had been more interested in receiving favors than giving them. But she had no trouble picturing herself peeling Gawen's pants down and worshiping his long shaft with her mouth. And she would have enjoyed every minute of it.

Nes cleared her throat when she realized she had been staring at Gawen's erection for an unreasonably long time. She let her gaze slowly trail up his abs and chest to his face, before meeting his heated gaze.

Pushing away her embarrassment at being caught admiring his package, she studied the big man. From this angle he could be mistaken for an angel, with his bright blue eyes and his almost white hair seeming to shine like a halo around his head. The only thing missing was a set of white feathery wings framing his muscular body. Calling him gorgeous was an understatement, and she already knew that she would miss his attention as soon as their performance was over, and they reverted to being mere acquaintances. If that was even possible after what they were about to embark on.

The truth was she would be avoiding him after this was over. It would be too awkward and painful to be around him after pretending to be his. At least staying away from him wouldn't be too difficult, considering she was living in Wick, and he would live with her brother's pack just north of Inverness.

His hand cupped her cheek as he smiled down at her. "Try to get some rest. We'll be busy putting our acting skills to the test once we get there."

Nodding, she obediently closed her eyes, missing his touch as soon as he removed his hand. Sleeping would be impossible with him so close when all she wanted to do was run her hands over his body and press her lips to his for another hot kiss.

Nes almost smiled when an idea formed in her mind. She might not be able to sleep, but she could pretend to be. And anything she did in her sleep couldn't be held against her, right?

Pulling in a deep breath, she let herself relax against him. A few minutes of calm, even breathing should be enough to let him think she was asleep, and anything she did after that, she could reasonably claim not to remember.

His thighs were thick and solid under her head, and her mind reverted to him sitting on his heels while pleasuring himself. His whole body had been tense, his muscles straining as the orgasm rocked his body. Her eyes had automatically focused on his thick cock jerking in his hand, but she had noticed the magnificence of the rest of his body as well. The sharp ridges of his abs, his sculpted chest and shoulders, bulging biceps, and thick powerful thighs. The man was truly a masterpiece with respect to the male physique.

Ever since seeing him like that, she hadn't been able to get him out of her mind. And her hands had been itching to glide over his solid muscles, to add texture to the visual image of him burned into her retinas.

When she thought enough time had gone by, she curled her body tighter and tucked her chin closer to her chest until her forehead was resting against the solid bulge in his pants.

Gawen let out a small gasp, and his thighs tensed. Several seconds went by before his muscles relaxed, and he let out a breath.

Nes had to concentrate not to burst out laughing at his reaction. Perhaps she was being a bit cruel to tease him like this, but after first sneaking up on her in the water and then blowing her mind with his amazing kiss, he was due a little payback.

***

Gawen

Gawen let his head drop back against the headrest and tried to concentrate on his breathing. Focusing his attention on the woman currently resting her head against his dick had been a mistake. It was bad enough having her forehead sliding against his erection with every curve in the road, but watching her soft lips so close to his swollen shaft while she was moving against him was worse.

This was not what he had planned when he suggested she lie down and get some rest. But it was too late to do anything about that now. If he tried to move her, she would wake up, and he didn't have the heart to do that when she obviously needed sleep.

Gawen fisted his hands when another curve caused her to move, and a spike of pleasure raced through him. He hadn't asked how long it would take them to get to Fearolc, and he didn't trust his voice enough to ask Trevor. But he already knew it would be longer than he liked, and he would undoubtedly stay hard the entire time. There was no way he would be able to relax with Nes nestled against his groin like she was.

The woman in question suddenly pulled in a sharp breath, and he looked down at her, hoping that it was a sign that she was waking up. But instead of opening her eyes, she lifted her hand and slid it across his thigh beneath her head until her pinky was nestled against his balls.

He jerked when his cock twitched and his balls tightened in anticipation of release. Except there would be no release, not until they reached their destination and he could find somewhere private to relieve the pressure building in his nuts.

Fuck. As much as he loved the thrill of having Nes so close, this was turning into a long edging session that was bordering on torture.

A bump in the road made him groan when her head grinded more firmly against him and nudged him closer to an orgasm. If he didn't manage to redirect his focus to something more mundane, he was going to blow right there in the backseat of Trevor's car, and that would be more than a little inappropriate.

Nes would surely be horrified to wake up to him filling his pants with his seed, and Trevor and his mate wouldn't be impressed either.

But what could he possibly focus on that would be interesting or terrible enough to keep his attention diverted from the beautiful black-haired woman in his lap and what she was doing to him?

He grabbed on to the only subject he could think of—Amber. If the nasty creature was allowed to live much longer, she might end up hurting or killing most of them, including Nes.

The thought sent what felt like a cold slurry of ice through his veins and doused some of his fiery need. Just the thought of Nes being in danger terrified him, and he would do anything in his power to protect her.

Pretending that they were about to be mated would put Amber's attention squarely on them, and since he was the most powerful of the two of them, Amber's primary target would most likely be Nes. He had to keep that in mind at all times and make sure Amber never got an opportunity to hurt his woman.

Gawen winced at his own choice of words, even if they were only in his mind. *His woman.* It was a tempting concept, but he was fully aware it would never be anything other than a hopeless dream.

The car suddenly swerved, and his hands grabbed onto Nes and held her firmly against him. Looking around them, he realized someone had pulled out into the road right in front of them, and Trevor had veered to avoid hitting them.

"Fucking asshole." The alpha wolf's shoulders were tense, and he slammed his hand against the steering wheel. "Some people shouldn't be allowed to drive at all."

A hand slapping against Gawen's chest made him look down—and freeze. His hand was cupping the back of Nes's head, pressing her face so firmly against his dick and lower belly that she couldn't breathe.

He let go of her, and she pulled her head back as she sucked in a breath.

"I'm sorry, I—"

"Was trying to choke me?" Wide eyes stared up at him. "What happened?"

"Someone pulled out into the road right in front of us, and Trevor had to swerve to avoid hitting their car." He studied her face, looking for any indication that she was angry with him and not just startled. "I just wanted to protect you, not suffocate you."

Her eyes dropped to his erection, a blush turning her cheeks rosy. "Um, sure. Perhaps I should just…" She pushed up from her horizontal position and moved around until she was sitting next to him.

Gawen didn't know what to say or do to alleviate the awkwardness between them. He had acted on pure instinct to make sure she stayed safe, and she seemed to understand that, but waking up with his hard cock in her face must have been a shock nevertheless.

As the seconds stretched in absolute silence, his heart gradually sank to the pit of his stomach. Things had been going well between them. She had been teasing him, and he had started to believe that their time together might turn out to be fun, even if he would be hurt when it was all over.

Of course you would believe that. Always so naive. When will you ever learn? He sighed and let his head tip forward in silent defeat. The voices were right. The reason he usually ended up disappointed or hurt was because he let his optimism rule him, conveniently forgetting his previous failures to make friends and connect with people.

His eyes shot open when a hand suddenly clasped his. Staring down at Nes's small hand tightening around his large one, he swallowed down the emotions that threatened to choke him. She was touching him, comforting him.

Gawen turned his head to look at her. She was staring straight ahead and wouldn't meet his gaze, but the small smile curving her lips made his heart flutter in his chest.

CHAPTER 10

Nes

"It feels like an eternity since we were here."

Jennie's statement made Nes pay more attention to the scenery outside. It was so lush and green, but so were most of the Scottish Highlands in summer.

"And yet it's no more than a few weeks." Trevor slowed the car and turned onto a gravel road. "A lot has happened in those weeks, though, both good and bad. But mostly good I think, considering how many have found their mates. It's like the universe has decided to do us some favors to compensate for the evil we're fighting."

Jennie laughed. "How poetic. I think of it more as random luck, but then what do I know? There is obviously more to this world than I had realized before I arrived in Scotland. Perhaps the universe has a mind of its own and suddenly went into a matchmaking phase. After what I have learned in the last few weeks, anything is possible really."

"Exploring new ideas for a novel, are you?" Trevor stopped the car outside a large house and shut off the engine before turning to smile at his mate. "I guess shifters and vampires aren't exotic enough for you anymore."

"You will always be exotic to me." Jennie leaned toward Trevor with her head tipped back like she wanted a kiss.

Nes averted her eyes and opened the door before loosening her grip on Gawen's hand. But he still held onto her, obviously not ready to let it go. Or perhaps it was just to keep up the illusion that they were more than friends.

Ever since she had taken his hand, they had been sitting quietly next to each other. She hadn't been able to come up with something to talk about, but it hadn't seemed to matter. The silence between them had been comfortable, like words weren't necessary.

Gawen followed close behind when she got out of the vehicle, and she turned to him as soon as he had straightened to his full height. She wasn't small for a woman, but he was still almost a head taller than her, and his muscular frame made him seem even bigger.

Before she could say anything, he pulled her close and kissed her forehead. "Thank you."

Pushing her brows together in confusion, she tipped her head back and stared up at him. "What for?"

His lips stretched into a smile. "For being you."

She wasn't sure what he meant by that, but she let it go with a smile and took a step back.

More cars pulled up and parked in front of the

main house, which was only one of several buildings making up the estate. The place looked well maintained and cared for.

Henry walked up to them, carrying Eleanor covered in a blanket to protect her from the sun. His smile widened when his gaze dipped to where Gawen and her hands were clasped. "You make it look so natural. Should I be worried that there's something going on between the two of you?" He winked at her, and she rolled her eyes at him.

"We're just doing what you asked of us, big brother." Nes gave him a sweet smile. "Or have you changed your mind?"

"Not at all." Henry grinned. "But I hadn't expected you to look so good together."

Nes felt heat creep up into her cheeks again. What was it with her and blushing all of a sudden? She didn't think she had ever blushed so much in her life as she had since she met Gawen, not even as an awkward teenager. But then she had never met anyone like the tall blond man before.

Thankfully, Trevor and his mate approached them and saved her from trying to come up with a neutral response to her brother.

"Are you ready to get a tour of the house?" Trevor indicated to follow him before turning and heading toward the entrance with Jennie in tow.

They all filed into the hallway, crowding the space. Gawen let go of her hand before putting an arm around her waist and pulling her close to his side.

Even if Amber happened to be close, she wouldn't have been able to see them where they were standing against the wall, but Nes didn't object to Gawen's closeness. Most likely he had decided to stay in character regardless of where they were or if they could be seen by someone outside the house. And she couldn't fault him for his decision. Slipping up would be less likely if they kept up the act at all times.

A shiver raced up her spine. They were supposed to be madly in love, and she already knew it would be easy to fall in love with this man. He was strong yet vulnerable, like he had lived through things he shouldn't have had to. Her childhood hadn't been the best, but at least she'd had a stable pack around her. Even with some emotional scars, she didn't feel like she was worse off than most other people. But she had a feeling Gawen couldn't boast the same.

"There are plenty of bedrooms upstairs and some on this level." Trevor's voice made her turn her head to look at the man standing by the stairs leading up to the second floor of the house. "Michael and Steph, you already have a bedroom on the ground floor, and Sabrina, I assume the bedroom you were given upstairs is big enough for you and Leith?"

The blond witch nodded before smiling up at her mate. "It is."

"Good." Trevor smiled. "Julianne, you will of course stay in Duncan's room this time."

Duncan laughed. "Obviously." Without warning he buried his face in the crook of his mate's neck, and Julianne squealed, swatting at him.

"All right." Trevor laughed and shook his head at Duncan's antics. "Then can you please find a room for Bryson and Fia on this level instead of torturing your mate?"

Duncan's head snapped up, a look of mock

indignation on his face. "Torturing? I'll have you know—"

"Yeah, yeah. Now do as you're told." Trevor's grin was wide, the man obviously enjoying yanking his friend's chain. "The rest of you who don't have a designated room, please follow me."

Henry, Eleanor, Callum, Vamika, and Aidan all moved toward the stairs.

Gawen took a step forward, and Nes let him lead her as they followed the others. She hadn't really considered the sleeping arrangements before they arrived, but based on what Sabrina had said about Amber being able to determine their location, Gawen would have to stay in a room close to hers.

They arrived in a long corridor upstairs, and Trevor led them down to the left before opening one of the doors lining the corridor and peering inside. "Henry and Eleanor, you can take this room. It's—"

"They have to share a room."

Everyone turned to stare as Sabrina hurried down the corridor toward them.

"I'd like to see the person who would try to separate us." Henry snorted.

"Not you." Lifting an eyebrow, Sabrina shook her head at Henry and sighed like he was being deliberately dense. "You." She turned her head and stared directly at Nes before moving her gaze to Gawen.

CHAPTER 11

Nes

Nes felt her eyes widen, and her spine stiffened in apprehension. She had agreed to play her part of a couple in love, but sleeping in the same room was taking it a bit too far. She had counted on having some time on her own to be able to cope with the strain of being close to Gawen the whole day.

"Okay." Gawen's agreement shook her out of her stunned silence and made her look up at him. "We can handle that."

No! Maybe you can, but I can't. She wanted to scream the words at him, at all of them. This was too much. How was she going to be able to maintain a healthy emotional distance from him if she had to spend one hundred percent of her time next to him? Not to mention lying next to him in a bed.

"Nes, do you agree?" There was concern in her brother's voice.

Swallowing hard, she met Henry's gaze. His brows were pushed together, and the corners of his lips were angled downward. *No, I don't.* But she couldn't say that and let everyone down. Sabrina wouldn't have asked them to share a room if it wasn't necessary.

Nes nodded, not trusting her voice enough to speak. Her heart was racing, and she desperately wanted some time alone to cool down and erect some kind of barrier between her heart and the world around her.

Henry didn't look convinced, so she swallowed to alleviate the tightness in her throat and returned her focus to Sabrina. "So, what you're saying is that we need to sleep within touching distance to be able to fool Amber. Otherwise, it would've been okay to have rooms next to each other, right?"

"That's correct." Sabrina nodded. "I don't know the accuracy with which Amber can tell where we are, but it seems to be fairly precise. I understand if it might be awkward for you two to stay in the same room, but if it's any consolation, you can sleep with your clothes on."

Nes breathed a silent sigh of relief at that. "Good to know." For some reason she hadn't considered clothes at all. Perhaps because the mere mention of Gawen and her sharing a room had brought up the image of him naked and pleasuring himself.

"Then let's find you a room." Trevor smiled before turning and heading farther down the corridor. "I think this one might be suitable." He opened a door on the right and walked inside.

Gawen let go of her, and she walked into the room ahead of him. The sight that met her made her smile.

The room was beautiful and filled with light. Long sheer white curtains framed a fantastic view of the green hills rising not far behind the house. The walls were painted a light coffee and cream color, and the floor was dark wood. Crisp white linen covered the huge bed.

"The bathroom is through that door." Trevor indicated a door to the right of where she had stopped a couple of feet from the entrance. "There should be fresh towels in there. If you need anything, just tell me or Duncan."

"Thank you." Gawen's deep voice sounded from right behind her, making a shiver of heat rush down her spine.

They would be staying in this room alone in the same bed with no one to make her think twice if she fell for the temptation to touch him. It was scary and exciting at the same time. How would he react if she undid his pants in the middle of the night and took his cock into her mouth? Would he push her away or welcome her attention? He hadn't pushed her away when she fondled him in the water before lunch, but that didn't mean he wouldn't remind her that this was all pretend if she got carried away.

"I'll leave you to it then." Trevor smiled as he passed her on his way out of the room.

Heat suffused her cheeks again when she realized she had been staring at the bed with who knew what kind of expression on her face. Had there been a hint of amusement in the alpha wolf's eyes? She wasn't sure, but she felt like she had been caught red-handed.

Walking over to the windows to take in the view, she silently berated herself for acting like a teenager with a crush. This wasn't the first time she had been attracted to someone, but it had never felt like this. And it was just her luck that the first person she could have seen herself settling down with was a shifter and therefore off-limits due to the whole mating issue.

Footsteps sounded from behind her, and she didn't have to turn around to know it was Gawen approaching her. "It's beautiful here." His voice was soft and smooth.

She wanted to lean back against him and let him hold her, but feeling his body against hers would only make this worse. "It is." A frustrated sigh slipped out before she could prevent it.

"But you're not happy you have to share a room with me."

Nes's shoulders tensed. *Shit.* She had hoped he hadn't picked up on her frustration, but of course he had. "I'm sorry. It's just… I just…" She gave up trying to find a way to explain herself without hurting him or admitting her own attraction to him. He might have already guessed how she was feeling, but she had no intention of spelling it out.

"I'm sorry." The dejection in his voice made her frown. "It's not too late to back out. We'll come up with another way to attract Amber's attention."

"No." She spun and put her hands on his chest. "We have to make this work. It might be the best chance we've got to lure her to us and kill her."

His expression was pensive while he studied her face for several seconds before saying anything. And if she wasn't mistaken, there was a shadow of hurt in his eyes. "You can trust me. We'll sleep fully clothed, and I promise not to touch you while we're in bed together."

Then he raised his gaze to stare out of the window behind her. "I can't promise I won't have an erection, though. I can't seem to help it around you. Just please don't feel threatened by it."

Nes felt her jaw slacken as she stared up at him. Heat settled low in her belly at the reminder of his hard cock. She'd seen it, touched it, and had it pressed against her face so far. And the last thing she had felt was threatened.

CHAPTER 12

Gawen

Gawen kept his gaze locked on the hills behind the estate. Nes had been shocked when she had learned that they had to share a room, but he wasn't sure why. He had expected as much, but for some reason she had thought they would be able to fool Amber while having separate bedrooms.

What he hadn't expected was how much her shock had affected him. The knowledge that she didn't want to stay in a room alone with him had been like a punch in the gut, making him question whether their game of pretend was such a good idea after all.

What would happen if they slipped up in front of Amber? It might provoke the bitch into killing Nes when she realized she had been tricked. And there was no way he could let that happen. He wouldn't allow the beautiful black-haired wolf to end up a sacrifice, not even to save Henry and his friends.

"I can't let you do this." He looked down, meeting her gaze. "I can't let you risk your life for—"

"Stop." She shook her head with a determined expression on her face. "I said I'll do this, and I will. We can make this work."

He shook his head right back at her. "No, I don't want you to. I'll talk to Trevor. Perhaps he knows someone else around here who would be willing to act as my mate-to-be."

Nes's eyes widened, and she took a step back. Her mouth opened like she was going to say something, but then she closed it again without making a sound.

Gawen gave her what he hoped was a genuine smile before he turned away from her. The last thing he wanted was to act like someone else's lover, but to keep Nes safe, he would do that and more. She was worth ten of him, easily.

"No!" Her sharp command made him stop, the word accompanied by a pulse of glorious power that shot straight to his shaft. "I won't allow it. You're... You and I will finish what we've started, and I won't take no for an answer."

He shuddered as happiness and need blended in a powerful mix and spread through his body, causing his cock to harden in misunderstood anticipation. Turning slowly, he took in her narrowed eyes and tight fists. "Whatever you say, little bird."

Objecting would have been safer for her, but he couldn't bring himself to do it. Not when she had used a direct command like that. He had no choice but to do what she wanted. And he would enjoy every moment of their time together.

Gawen smiled when he guided Nes into the living room with a hand on the small of her back. Most of the others were already there for what he had been told would be a meeting to plan their next moves.

People were standing around talking. The only exceptions were Callum and Vamika, who were sitting next to each other on a couch working on their laptops.

Henry and Eleanor were talking to Duncan and Julianne, and judging by the frowns on their faces, the topic was Amber. Sabrina, Steph, and Fia were gathered in a small group, probably trying to come up with ways to combine their magic to restrain the evil witch.

"Good. Looks like everyone is here."

Gawen turned to see Trevor walking into the room, holding Jennie's hand, and with Aidan right behind them.

"We have a party to plan and a witch to catch." The estate owner grinned as he swung his gaze around the room. "I can't wait to put the bitch down. It's about fucking time. And this time we're going to do it."

Gawen took Nes's hand in his, tightening his grip. He wasn't nearly as confident about their ability to stop Amber, but he was prepared to do whatever necessary to make it happen. Except risking Nes's life. If he sensed she was in any immediate danger, he would act accordingly, no matter if that jeopardized their chances of destroying the witch.

"Why don't you all take a seat so we can get started?" Trevor moved over to one of the couches and sat down, pulling Jennie down next to him and putting an arm around her shoulders.

The rest of them found seats in the various chairs and sofas around the room. Nes sat down in a chair, and Gawen pulled up a chair to sit beside her. He would have preferred to have her sitting close to him on a couch, but with the way they had been touching almost constantly since they left Leith's house, he wasn't surprised that she wanted to put a little space between them.

Glancing at the line of windows in the room, he frowned. He didn't expect Amber to be on the estate yet, since it wasn't long since they'd arrived themselves. But he could be wrong. She was unpredictable, and he wouldn't put anything past her.

Like Nes had read his mind, she reached over and braided her fingers with his. Smiling, he looked down at her hand. What he wouldn't give for this act between them to be real. To have Nes fall in love with him and agree to become his mate. He was fully aware that it was foolish wishful thinking, but he couldn't help the way his heart sped up with every one of her smiles and touches. And the kiss they had shared had caused his whole body to practically vibrate with his longing for her.

"So, by party I assume you're talking about the celebration of our mating?" Nes's tone was so matter of fact that Gawen turned to stare at her face. It was less than half an hour since she had balked at sharing a room with him, but here she was speaking of their pretend mating like it didn't bother her at all.

They hadn't discussed when the supposed mating was to take place yet. It would have to be within a few days to be believable since shifters usually mated almost immediately after the decision was made, but they had to allow some time to alert Amber to what was about to happen.

Trevor nodded. "Yes. And it should take place tomorrow, which means we have to find a way to make Amber aware of the event as soon as possible. Any ideas?"

The room went quiet, and there were a lot of pondering expressions around the room.

Gawen hadn't given the issue much thought, having been too busy thinking about Nes and the role they were playing in the upcoming events. He wasn't good with computers or any other electronic devices for that matter, so if there was some kind of digital solution to this issue, he wouldn't be the one to think of that.

"We have her phone number, and even though Amber only rarely turns it on, we can send her a text." There was a frown on Callum's face as he sighed. "But I haven't been able to come up with a suitable message that doesn't sound like an outright invitation."

Gawen frowned as a thought bloomed in his mind. What if the answer wasn't the use of modern technology, but the use of ancient magic? Amber was a witch, after all, and as far as he had heard, her tool in fighting them had always been magic. Her main reason for what she was doing might be revenge, but her desire for power was just as prominent.

"What if we show her an enticing display of our combined power?" He looked at Aidan before moving his gaze to Fia, Sabrina, and Steph in turn. "Amber might perceive it as a threat aimed at herself and her daughter, but I bet her desire to harness that power will outweigh any apprehension she might feel. We can make it seem like most of the power comes from me, and the fact that I intend to take a mate will let Amber know that she can easily take my power if she is present at the mating. She won't be able to resist the opportunity."

"What do you mean by display?" Aidan's brows pulled together as he leaned forward in his seat and rested his elbows on his knees. "Sending her a video or finding a way to reach her with our magic? The first one is easy but might be dismissed as fake or a trap. The second one would be impossible to ignore, but I'm not sure if it's feasible."

"I'd be happy to try the second option." Steph's mouth curved in a smile. "Sabrina can locate people who are far away, so there has to be a way to send a magical message, so to speak, if we all work together."

Michael's jaw clenched, and he pulled his mate tighter against his side. "It sounds like something that can go horribly wrong. That amount of combined power requires a lot of control, or you might end up setting off the magical equivalent of a nuclear bomb."

Chuckling, Steph turned to look at her mate with love softening her eyes. "I love that you're worried about me and everyone else. But no matter what we do, there will be a risk of getting hurt or even killed. With what we've been through in the last few weeks, we're lucky we're all still here. And if we want to keep it that way, we need to lure Amber into our trap and kill her."

Michael's lips pressed together in a hard line, but he didn't say anything. Gawen got the impression it wasn't the first time the man was obliged to let his mate do something dangerous.

"Between us I think we have a lot of power and a lot of control." Gawen returned his gaze to Aidan. "I'm more uncertain about our ability to reach Amber and give her an intelligible message."

The enforcer nodded. "Yes, I agree. But nothing is impossible. Even at my age I keep discovering new abilities among witches and supernaturals. The world is ever-changing. What seemed utopic yesterday is routine tomorrow. And the other way around is true too."

Sabrina suddenly stood, causing Leith to scramble to get up as well, surprise widening his eyes. "Let's give it a try." The blond witch smiled. "My power has increased since I transitioned and mated Leith, and I for one would like to find out if this is possible."

"I'm in." Fia tried to get up, but Bryson tightened his arm around her, effectively keeping her locked against him.

"Redbird, please rethink this." The panther alpha's brown eyes darkened with concern. "If anything were to happen to you, I—"

Fia turned her head and pressed her lips against her mate's, effectively silencing him. Pulling back, she grinned at him. "Now let me get to work, Bry."

The big man huffed in irritation but let her go.

"I think the garden would be a suitable venue for our experimentation." Aidan rose and crossed his arms over his chest. "The rest of you should stay here just in case. You can keep an eye on us from the windows if you'd like."

"Like hell I will," Bryson grumbled and grabbed Fia's hand. "She's mine to protect. I'll let you work, but I'll stay close the whole time."

"Amen to that." Leith nodded his agreement.

Nes's grip on Gawen's hand tightened, and he turned to look at her. Her eyes were wide and fixed on Leith, like the man's words had frightened her.

"You should stay here with the others." Gawen gave Nes a soft smile when she turned her head to stare at him. "There won't be much to see. Magic in itself isn't visible, only the effects of it are. But this will only be us trying to meld our powers, so hopefully, there won't be any visible signs of what we're doing at all."

Her eyes narrowed. "What do you mean hopefully?"

He shrugged. "Exactly what it sounds like, that I hope you can't see any signs that we're using our magic. If you do, something has gone wrong."

Nes sucked her bottom lip into her mouth and chewed on it while studying his face. If he wasn't mistaken, she was worried about him, and the realization almost made him smile. It didn't mean she had any romantic feelings for him, but it still felt good to have her care enough that she let her concern for him show.

Aidan headed toward the door, and Gawen loosened his grip on Nes's hand. It took her a second to let go of him, and she did it with an almost inaudible sigh.

After giving her a warm smile, he rose and followed the other magically inclined people. Thankfully, Nes hadn't insisted on joining them in the garden. And he hoped she didn't change her mind about staying in the house. Michael and the other mates' concern wasn't unfounded. They were five people with strong magic, and trying to combine their power had the potential to go horribly wrong.

CHAPTER 13

Nes

Nes stared at Gawen's broad back as he followed Aidan, the witches, and their mates out of the room. Worry gnawed in her stomach, urging her to go after him and keep an eye on him. But he wanted her to stay away, and she wasn't his real girlfriend, so it would seem strange if she insisted on being present when she could easily observe from the safety of the house.

Turning her head, she let her gaze glide over the remaining people in the room until it crashed with her brother's. The smirk on his face told her that he had been watching her for a while and had picked up on her unease.

Henry was welcome to think whatever he wanted. She had no intention of coming up with any excuses for her behavior. And if he made any comments about her poorly hidden feelings, she would make sure to tell him who was really to blame for her being there and utilizing her nonexistent acting skills to attract a killer witch.

After rising from the comfortable leather chair, she turned to look out the window. The five people with magical abilities gathered in a circle on the lawn about ten yards from the house. Gawen was standing between Sabrina and Steph, and Nes studied his profile as he listened to Aidan speak.

Nes couldn't make out the words through the closed windows, and she frowned and gritted her teeth in irritation. She wanted to be prepared if something happened to Gawen, but how could she when she had next to no knowledge of magic and how it worked?

"I'm sure he'll be fine."

She jerked at Henry's soft voice not far from her ear. Glaring up at him, she bit back her admonishment of him sneaking up on her. He deserved a well-placed punch to the gut, but that would only serve to confirm his suspicion that she was more worried about Gawen than the rest of the people out there.

Returning her attention to the people outside, she pulled in a calming breath. "I hope they know what they're doing, is all. I wouldn't like to see any of them hurt."

"I'm sure Aidan will do everything he can to control their combined power." Trevor had moved to stand in front of the window to the left, his arms wrapped protectively around Jennie. "And knowing him they'll start off nice and easy to get a feel for each other's magic before they try anything requiring more power and precision."

Nes nodded slowly. *Please let that be true.* As much as she hoped they would find a way to reach Amber with their message, she couldn't help cursing Gawen for coming up with the idea to try something so dangerous.

Several minutes went by while Aidan kept talking, only momentarily pausing when one of the others spoke. Leith, Michael, and Bryson were standing off to the side watching, and judging by their tight expressions, they weren't feeling any happier about the proceedings than they had before.

Fuck this. Nes took a step back, ready to throw caution to the wind and walk out there to be close to Gawen, when the five people in the circle clasped hands and closed their eyes.

She stopped and studied each of their faces for any signs of discomfort, but there was nothing. They looked calm, like whatever they were trying to do wasn't requiring a lot of effort.

Did that mean that this was easier than they had thought? Or hadn't they started yet, and all she was witnessing was some kind of meditation phase. Perhaps they needed to empty their minds of intrusive thoughts before they could concentrate on the task at hand.

Nes suddenly wished she'd had more time to ask questions about magic and how it worked. But apart from a few questions during dinner the night before, she had no knowledge of what these people could do. And with the way her mind and body had been otherwise occupied since meeting Gawen, it wasn't a surprise that the existence of magic hadn't sparked more of an interest.

A distant rumbling sound suddenly caught her attention, and her heart rate sped up until she realized what she was hearing. Thunder.

Letting out a relieved breath, she smiled at her own anxiety. For a second there she had thought the rumbling sound was created by the circle of powerful people outside, but thankfully, that wasn't the case.

Five more minutes went by, and Nes's body was starting to relax with the uneventful display outside. With the mate's concern about the use of magic, she had expected there to be at least some visible evidence of what was going on. But this show was turning out to be remarkably boring.

The sky suddenly darkened, and she became aware of the thick dark clouds that filled the eastern sky and were quickly heading their way.

Nes cocked her head and frowned as she stared at the threatening clouds. Having weather like that roll in from the sea in the west would have been nothing out of the ordinary, but it seemed strange that it would cross the mountains from the east. But who was she to tell what was normal in these parts?

"Those are ominous-looking clouds." The concern in Trevor's voice made Nes turn to look at him. "And they completely defy what everyone knows around here that easterly is synonymous with dry and sunny weather."

Jennie lifted her gaze to her mate, her eyes wide. "What do you mean by that? You almost make it sound like it's unnatural."

Trevor pulled in a deep breath before letting it out slowly. His eyes studied the dark clouds like he could somehow find the reason for their existence in the way they moved. "I only know of one person who can control the weather, and he's thousands of miles away.

It's hard to know what to believe at the moment, but I don't like what I'm seeing."

Nes's spine stiffened. So, she had been right about her concern. There was something odd about those clouds. "Does Amber have the ability to affect the weather?"

"Not as far as we know." The owner of the estate tightened his hold around his mate. "But she keeps surprising us, so who am I to say what she can and can't do?"

Staring at the clouds, Nes swallowed hard. The thick mass was almost upon them, creating a wall of rain that was racing toward them with promises of a storm. But she hadn't seen any lightning or heard any thunder since that first distant rumble.

Movement to her right drew her attention to Duncan leaning in close to the window to the right and staring up at the sky. "Perhaps it's just the result of the unusual stretch of hot weather we've had this summer. Usually we get rain regularly, but there's hardly been a drop for weeks. I think it's about time we got a proper downpour. God knows we need it."

"You might be right." Trevor nodded, and his shoulders visibly relaxed. "This summer has been unusually hot and dry."

Jennie reached out toward the window, both palms facing the glass but not quite touching it. "You can almost feel the electricity crackling in the air. I've only felt that once before, down by the sea loch not long after I first arrived here. Right before you kissed me for the first time." She turned her head to look up at her mate with love shining in her blue eyes.

A bright flash seared Nes's retinas, and a

resounding boom brought her hands up to cover her ears against the painfully loud noise.

CHAPTER 14

Nes

Nes blinked her eyes several times before her vision started to return, but it was still a few more seconds before she could see well enough to make out the people around her. They had all moved several steps back from the windows, and they all looked just as shocked and disoriented as she was.

Gawen. Nes's already elevated heart rate picked up another notch as she closed the distance to the window.

He wasn't there.

Each of the three couples out there had found each other and was checking each other over to make sure they were okay. But neither Gawen nor Aidan was anywhere in sight.

Nes spun and raced toward the door, almost crashing into Aidan when he suddenly appeared in the doorway right in front of her. She stepped to the side to squeeze past him but stopped when Gawen appeared right behind the enforcer.

Her pretend mate-to-be's white-blond hair was messy, and his eyes looked a bit wild, but apart from that he looked fine.

Their eyes met, and Nes pulled in a deep breath as she felt herself start to relax.

"Who has the ability to deflect lightning?" Aidan's sharp voice from right next to her made her snap her head around to gawk at him. What had he just said?

"I felt someone push that lightning away. Good thing they did, too, because otherwise it would have struck the house." Aidan's different-colored eyes wandered around the room, staring at each person in turn.

Henry frowned. "Why do you think it was someone in here? It must have been Gawen or one of the witches surely." Her brother's gaze moved from Aidan to where Gawen was still standing in the doorway. "Was it you?"

Before Gawen could answer, Aidan shook his head firmly. "It was someone in here. I felt it. But I couldn't tell who, and I still can't detect someone with that kind of power in here. It's a very unusual ability, one I would only expect to find with a very powerful supernatural or witch."

Nes scanned the faces of the people standing around the room, but the look of confusion was unanimous. Was it possible that someone didn't know they had that kind of ability and had just used it without realizing what they were doing? It seemed impossible.

Fat drops of rain hit the windows and quickly

escalated until it sounded like they were in the middle of a gun range.

An arm slid around her waist, and a smile tugged at the corner of her lips when she realized who it was. Gawen's large hand settled on her hip before pulling her close to his side.

"I'm glad to see you're all right, little bird." Gawen's deep voice was soft next to her ear, and she doubted that anyone else had heard him above the noise of the hammering rain.

"You too." She smiled up at him. "You were more at risk out there than I was in here."

Trevor walked up to Aidan. "I felt something too, but"—he shook his head with a deep frown marring his forehead—"it was confusing." His gaze slid to Jennie standing next to him with her hand in his.

The enforcer nodded before letting his gaze glide around the room. "I would like to touch each one of the shifters who were inside at the time of the lightning strike to see if I can detect the power used to deflect it. I assume since no one has come forward that the person isn't aware of their ability."

"Not the humans?" Jennie looked up at Aidan before turning her head to meet Julianne's gaze.

Aidan shook his head with a small smile as he considered the blond human in front of him. "No, I don't think that would be necessary. A human wouldn't be able to harness that kind of power without being aware of it. Shifters don't usually have abilities like that either, but a rare few has something extra in addition to their normal shifter power, and I believe one of you does." His gaze landed on Trevor.

"You can start with me." The owner of the house

let go of his mate's hand and squared his shoulders. "But I'm quite sure I'm not the person you're looking for. I know I'm powerful, but that's just my alpha power and nothing special."

Without saying anything, Aidan reached out and put his hand on Trevor's chest just above the V of the neckline of his shirt. Staring into the other man's eyes, the enforcer stilled.

It only lasted for a few seconds before Aidan pulled back and shook his head. "No, it's not you."

"I told you." Trevor smiled and took a step back. "Who's next?"

One after the other of the shifters came forward, and Aidan repeated the procedure with each one of them without results.

Nes was the last one to approach the enforcer. After pulling away from Gawen, she positioned herself in front of the exceptionally powerful man to let herself be examined like the others.

Aidan's gaze bored into hers as he put his hand against her chest with his fingertips touching her throat. His power immediately penetrated her skin and sank into her body, but it wasn't startling or uncomfortable.

After a few seconds, he pulled back and shook his head like he had with the others. "No, it isn't you either." He let out a frustrated sigh and ran a hand through his hair. "I don't understand. It shouldn't be possible to hide a power like that. I know one of you has the ability, but I can't detect it. I can't even feel it in the room with us, even though I know it came from this area of the house. It's like the ability just disappeared after it was used to save us all from harm."

During Aidan's examination of everyone who had been inside, the remaining people who had been gathered outside had entered the room and been informed of what was going on.

Leith stepped forward. "Perhaps it would be best if you checked the rest of us as well just to be sure. I know you claim you felt it come from the house, but with the power the five of you were using at the time, there might have been some interference."

Nes watched as Aidan nodded slowly before putting his hand on Leith's chest, but the result was the same as for the people who had been tested before him.

Sabrina narrowed her eyes at Aidan when Leith moved to the side, and the enforcer's gaze landed on her. "What will happen when you touch me this time? Will you shock me again like you did when we shook hands in Inverness?"

Leith's head snapped around, and he stared at her with wide eyes until some kind of realization made his mouth curve into a small smile. "I had completely forgotten about that."

Aidan chuckled. "I honestly don't know. And if you recall, I didn't feel anything last time, only you did. So perhaps it was all you."

"I doubt that." The blond witch raised an eyebrow at the man in front of her and crossed her arms over her chest. "I've never experienced anything like that with anyone else, so it's unlikely it came from me when you are the most powerful of the two of us."

The enforcer burst out laughing. "Well, there's only one way to find out, isn't there? Will you allow me to touch you?"

A couple of seconds went by before she nodded and stepped forward. "Okay."

Aidan raised his hand, and the whole room went quiet while everyone waited to see what was going to happen. Even the rain abated, the sound reducing to a soft whisper.

The enforcer's palm landed on Sabrina's chest, and Nes held her breath as she stared unblinking at the woman's face.

But there was no sign that the witch felt anything out of the ordinary at the contact, and a second later she smiled. "Nothing. I don't know what you did last time, but it didn't happen now."

Aidan let his hand rest against her skin for another few seconds before he pulled back and smiled. "I don't know for sure what happened when I met you in Inverness, but I have a suspicion."

"Which is?" Sabrina stared at him.

"Your body was pushing you to mate so you would start your transformation into a mermaid. It—"

"What?" Leith practically shouted the word as he took a step forward, just as Sabrina's head snapped back with a gasp like she had been struck in the face.

Aidan's brows pushed together in a frown as his gaze darted between the two people in front of him. "I assumed you had heard that by now. But I guess you haven't had time to confront your family about what they should have told you years ago, Sabrina?"

"I would've transformed when I mated." The blond witch had gone pale, making her blue eyes seem larger and darker than they usually did. "So that whole dying thing wasn't necessary for me to gain my true form?"

Nodding slowly, the enforcer's lips twitched like he had just tasted something sour. "Correct. And you should've already been aware of that."

"Fuck!" Leith's face tightened with rage, his eyes turning a shimmering emerald.

CHAPTER 15

Nes

Nes couldn't help but stare at Leith's shining eyes. Except for the color, they reminded her of how Gawen's eyes would shine when he was aroused. Did that mean Gawen was a similar kind of supernatural to Leith?

"I don't think my family knows what I am or that it was even a possibility. We're a family of witches, nothing more." Sabrina's voice was so soft it was almost inaudible. "Is that plausible?" Her eyes were pleading when she stared at Aidan.

The enforcer cocked his head in thought. "It is, but very unusual. Normally, there is a mermaid in every generation, but not always in a direct line. Your aunt could have been the last one and perhaps your grandmother's sister before that. If both of them died before they transformed, I suppose the family might have assumed the heritage was lost and decided not to disclose the information to your generation."

"I have both." Sabrina sighed and leaned into Leith's chest when he wrapped his arms around her.

"What do you mean, my angel?" Leith's eyes had reverted to their normal green color, but there was a tension in his jaw that spoke of his lingering anger.

"Both an aunt and a great aunt who died when they were no more than a couple of years old. It is likely that they were the mermaids of their generation."

Aidan nodded. "Quite possibly, but I suggest you speak to your family about that. If only to make sure someone in the next generation doesn't go through what you have."

"I will." Sabrina visibly swallowed. "I don't want anyone else to go through what we did." She lifted her head to meet her mate's gaze. "I don't want anyone to suffer like you did when you thought I was gone forever."

"My normal response to a statement like that would be to say that I have experienced worse." Leith let out a shaky breath. "But the truth is I have not, and I hope I never will. It is an experience I do not even wish upon my worst enemy."

Gawen's grip tightened on Nes's hip, but she didn't look up at him. Did she mean something to him? Would he grieve if something happened to her, beyond what was normal when losing an acquaintance? He'd already said he was happy to see she was all right, but that was nothing more than what you would typically say to a friend after a scary experience.

She bit the inside of her cheek and pushed the thoughts away. Why was she even contemplating this? Their talking and touching were nothing more than choreographed movements in a play. None of it meant anything. And when it was all over, they would go their separate ways. He would probably end up with a mate, and she—she wouldn't. The thought left her cold.

"But wait." Sabrina turned her head to look at Aidan. "What happens to a mermaid who falls in love with a human? Then there's no mating to initiate the transformation."

Aidan's eyes warmed. "Mating isn't specifically required to change, but love is. If the couple truly love each other, the transformation will start soon after they consummate their relationship."

"That's a relief." Sabrina's worried expression smoothed into a soft smile. "Thank you, Aidan. I have a lot more questions but perhaps we'll have some time to talk later."

"I'd be happy to." Aidan smiled at Leith and Sabrina before moving his gaze to Michael and Steph, who were standing a few feet to the left.

The examination of Michael, Steph, Bryson, and Fia didn't produce any other results than for the rest of them, and Nes had just concluded that they might never find out who had the unusual ability when Aidan turned to look at Gawen. For some reason the thought that the big man next to her might be the one Aidan was looking for hadn't crossed her mind.

A sense of loss filled her when Gawen let go of her hip and moved away. But she mentally waved the feeling away. It wasn't like they were one of the happy couples in the room, and she had to be careful not to get too accustomed to his attention.

Gawen stood in front of Aidan, and the enforcer

repeated the procedure he had used with all the rest of them. Except this time Aidan's brows shut up as soon as his palm connected with Gawen's skin.

Nes stared at Aidan's face, waiting for him to say something to explain the shocked expression on his face. But the seconds stretched, and no words were spoken.

After pulling his hand away, Aidan kept studying Gawen's face for several seconds before he finally opened his mouth. "I don't believe you have the ability to deflect lightning, but I couldn't say with absolute certainty. I've never come across someone like you before, and considering your young age, I believe you have potential abilities that are not developed yet. I don't know if you've told people here what you are, or if you even know the extent of what you are, but there might come a time when the enforcers will call upon you for assistance. If you don't mind."

Gawen's eyes were wide when he stared at Aidan. "Of...of course not. I'd be happy to help."

"Good. Thank you." Aidan gave a sharp nod before swinging his gaze around the room. "Unfortunately, we're no closer to finding the person who is much more powerful than they think they are. But we can come back to that later. Let's give ourselves a few minutes, and then I think we should get back to what we were trying to do when the storm hit."

Nes's heart was slamming hard against her ribs. There had been no doubt in her mind that Gawen was special, but special didn't seem to be an adequate word to describe what he truly was.

As far as she had been told, Leith was one of the

most powerful supernaturals in Scotland. And the enforcer easily surpassed Leith in power. But based on Aidan's description, Gawen had to be at least as powerful as Leith if not more so.

How the gorgeous blond man wasn't surrounded with women who wanted to be his mate she had no idea. But it wouldn't take long for that to happen once people realized his full potential. Beautiful women would be fighting for his attention, giving him a vast choice of suitable mates that were willing to do anything to get him.

Tears pricked the back of her eyes, and she took a couple of steps back before she turned and snuck out into the hallway. The thought of him with another woman sent daggers into her heart, the pain threatening to send her to her knees.

Stupid woman. What's wrong with you? Anger surged through her, easing her pain. She didn't want a mate. She had grown up knowing exactly what mating could do to someone, and that wasn't going to be her life. Mating and love weren't the same thing, but even love could turn sour after a while.

"Nes, are you all right?"

Henry's voice made her body tense. Silently cursing under her breath, she forced her shoulders back down and pasted a smile on her face before turning to face him.

"Yes. I guess this might be everyday stuff for you by now, but it's not for me." She let out a laugh that sounded too shrill in her own ears. "I just needed a moment alone to process everything."

His frown stayed in place while he scrutinized her face. Then his eyes softened, and he smiled. "I don't think this is everyday stuff for anyone. Or perhaps for Aidan. But the rest of us are just trying to cope the best we can. Hopefully, this will all be over soon, and we can return to our normal lives."

Her stomach lurched, and she winced. *Yes, and that should be a comforting thought and not something I dread.*

Nes nodded enthusiastically to try to cover her reaction. "I can't wait."

CHAPTER 16

Gawen

Gawen was sitting in a big leather armchair in the corner of the living room. He had chosen it on purpose, since it was the only seat that was located at a good distance from the couches and other chairs in the room, giving him an excuse not to interact with anyone.

After Aidan's words about him, he had felt everyone's eyes on him almost like ants crawling all over his body. They wanted to know what he was, and he couldn't blame them. He would have been curious, as well, if Aidan had told someone else they were one of a kind.

But Gawen couldn't bring himself to explain. The fear of seeing their expressions change with disappointment and disgust made his throat clog up. It was difficult enough to breathe, let alone try to speak.

He glanced at the door again, but there was no sign

of Nes. She had left the room soon after Aidan gave his description, and it hadn't felt right to follow her. Not when he had no idea why she'd left.

The enforcer had spoken like Gawen's uniqueness was something positive, perhaps even something to be admired. But in his experience that wasn't how it worked in shifter society. Unique meant different, and different was unacceptable.

Was that why Nes had left the room? After realizing how different he truly was? It wasn't like he had expected her to want to embark on a real relationship with him, but he had still nurtured a small hope that she would want to spend time with him after their fight with Amber was over.

"Are you ready to try again?"

Aidan's question brought him out of his thoughts, and he lifted his head to meet the man's gaze. After giving a short nod, he pushed up from the chair.

Once again they left the living room and continued out into the garden. The rain had passed, and the ground squished under their feet. The sky was still cloudy and dark, and another downpour might start at any time. But that was a risk they would have to take if they wanted to practice combining their magic.

Gawen sighed, his shoulders slumping. He had been eager to find a way to send a message to Amber before, but with everything that had happened since the first time they tried, he had lost his motivation. And his conviction that it must be possible had dwindled to a faint memory.

"Okay, let's continue where we left off last time." The smile in Aidan's voice drew Gawen's eyes to him. "We managed to meld our magic reasonably well together and let it simmer between us like an invisible ball of power. Let's do the same thing now. But when it's stable, I want you to work together to carefully aim it at the large rock over there and carve a large A into the side." Aidan's smile broadened into a grin, clearly prepared to take the credit if this worked out as planned.

The others laughed, but all Gawen could produce was a weak smile. He didn't belong with these people. They were so much better than he was. Strong and confident, and securely mated. Apart from himself, the only one who wasn't in a loving relationship was Aidan, but that man didn't seem to need a mate to boost his confidence and make him happy.

Hands gripped his, and he blinked his eyes when he realized he had momentarily lost focus. *Concentrate. All you have to do is control your power. You can do this.*

He pulled in a deep breath as he gathered his power. Then, he slowly breathed out while braiding his magic with the magic he felt pouring from the others. Sensing the growing ball of power at the center of the five-person circle, he worked to meld his magic more tightly with the others, creating something stronger and more homogenous in the process.

His eyes were closed in concentration, but he knew the product of their efforts was invisible. Nes might be watching, but she wouldn't be able to tell what they were doing, what *he* was doing. And from inside the house, she wouldn't even feel anything.

If only she could have seen what was happening, that he was making an effort to save everyone from Amber. Then she might have had a reason to admire him—to want him.

Magic slammed against his chest, searing his skin and forcing all the air out of his lungs. He was knocked backward. The back of his neck and shoulders hit the ground with a thud before the momentum flipped him over onto his front. He ended up with his face buried in the wet grass and water soaking into the front of his shirt and pants.

After rolling his head to the side, he pulled in a breath to fill his deflated lungs. His chest burned when it expanded and pulled at his charred skin, the pain enough to make his stomach roll with nausea.

"Gawen." Strong hands gripped his shoulders and rolled him over onto his back.

He gasped with pain when his damaged skin split. His body was already healing, but it would take a little while before it was back to normal.

"Fuck! That's a nasty burn."

If Gawen hadn't been in so much pain, he would have laughed at the distaste in Bryson's voice. The brawny, tattooed alpha clearly didn't like the sight of burned flesh. Or perhaps he just remembered what had happened to his own mate when she fought Amber in the clearing in Queen Elizabeth Forest Park.

He forced his eyes open and stared up at Bryson and Leith crouching next to him. "I'll be fine…in a few minutes." His voice was little more than a whisper.

"Minutes?" Leith shook his head slowly. "I believe it will take a little longer than that."

"Shit." Steph peered down at him from where she had come to stand next to his head. "I'm not sure I can help you with how close that wound is to your heart."

"It's okay." Gawen pulled in a shaky breath. "Just

give me a few minutes. Is everyone else all right?"

Bryson nodded. "Yes, you're the only one who's hurt."

He had just closed his eyes to focus on his healing when he heard someone running across the wet lawn. "Gawen." A soft hand cupped his cheek.

CHAPTER 17

Gawen

The shock and worry in Nes's voice made Gawen smile and peel his eyes open to stare into her wide dark-blue orbs. Her gentle touch was enough to increase his energy level and give his healing a boost.

"Damn, that's impressive." Bryson's eyebrows lifted as he stared at Gawen's chest. "I've never seen a wound heal that quickly before."

"Neither have I." Steph shook her head slowly with a look of awe on her face.

Nes didn't look impressed or relieved, though. "What happened? I know you said something could go wrong, but..."

He took in her furrowed brows and the tension in her body. Scaring her hadn't been his intention, and he had no plans to do it again, but it still warmed his heart to see her concern for him. She could have just stayed in the house and let the others take care of him. But she hadn't; she had come running to check on him.

"I lost concentration." He sighed and averted his eyes. "I owe you all an apology. This was all my fault, but at least I'm the only one who suffered for it."

"Can you help me bring him inside?" Nes's voice was suddenly stern and efficient. "He needs time to heal and some new clothes."

Gawen's gaze snapped back to hers. "No, I'll be—"

"No!" Her hard tone brooked no argument. "Your wound might be healing exceptionally fast, but that doesn't mean you don't need a break. You lost concentration and were seriously hurt because of it. What do you think will happen next time?"

"I…" He didn't know what to say. She had a point, but he couldn't tell her that the reason he had lost focus was because he had been thinking about her and how much he wanted her to like him. And instead of impressing her like he had wished, he had shown how careless and incompetent he was.

Bryson leaned forward and put a hand on his leg like he was preparing to lift him into his arms, but Gawen held up a hand and shook his head. "I can walk."

"Gawen." Nes's voice was colored by disapproval.

But instead of focusing on her, he pushed off the ground and sat up. His face twisted with discomfort, but looking down at his chest revealed that the wound was almost closed. The scabs covered a significant portion of his chest, but it wouldn't be long before those were replaced by smooth unblemished skin.

"Stubborn man." Nes's eyes were narrow when he met her gaze.

His mouth twitched with amusement, and she

pressed her lips together. She clearly wasn't happy with him, but instead of making him sad or weary, he reveled in the feeling. This reminded him of how a loving couple would act in this situation, and it sent frissons of happiness sparking through him.

Gawen rose to his feet, and no sooner had he straightened his spine than Nes grabbed his hand and pulled him toward the house. She didn't turn to look at him as she hurried toward the house, and it was probably a good thing, since he wasn't sure she would approve of the ridiculous grin on his face.

They entered the house, but instead of taking him to the living room like he had expected, she led him toward the stairs. His heart rate kicked up as he followed her upstairs before turning down the corridor toward their bedroom.

He wanted to ask her what she was thinking but refrained for fear of destroying his chance to be alone with her.

After leading him across the threshold, she let go of his hand and pointed toward the bed without looking at him. "Lie down and rest. I know you probably think you're invincible like most male shifters, but the fact that you lost focus and got hurt says otherwise."

He frowned and studied her profile. Her jaw was set, and she stared defiantly toward the windows. "I don't think I'm invincible, I just didn't sleep well last night." It was the truth even if it wasn't the reason he had fucked up.

A blush crept up her throat and into her cheeks, and she visibly swallowed before she turned her head away. "Lie down, Gawen." Her voice had a slight tremor to it.

Had she just remembered walking in on him jerking off? He should feel bad about that, but after the way she had touched his cock in the water right before lunch, he considered them to be even on that score. "Only if you lie down next to me so I can talk to you. I think we need to decide on the details of our pretend whirlwind romance." He couldn't prevent the smile that curved his lips.

Her head swirled around, and wide eyes met his. "You need to rest, not…" She bit her lip, looking decidedly uncomfortable.

"Not what?" He gave her what he hoped was a sexy smile and closed the distance between them until he was towering over her. "Don't you want to discuss our relationship and what we can do to convince Amber that we're fucking each other's brains out every chance we get?"

Nes's mouth fell open, and her eyes stayed glued to his as she tipped her head back and leaned a little backward. "I…" She licked her lips. "That's…"

He bent his head until his lips brushed the shell of her ear before he whispered, "I won't touch you. Not unless you ask me to." *But by fuck I want to.* Pushing into her velvet heat would be nothing short of heaven, and hearing her cry out with pleasure would be even better.

His shaft thickened, and his balls chose that moment to remind him that he had been hard several times since his last release.

"What if I ask you to?" Her voice was breathless.

His cock twitched, and he pulled his head back slowly until he could stare into her beautiful eyes. She blinked a couple of times but didn't look away. "I would take that as an invitation to worship your body. Do you want that?"

CHAPTER 18

Nes

Nes could hardly breathe as she stared into Gawen's glowing eyes. She wanted to believe him. That sex with him would be better. But the nagging voice at the back of her head was insisting that fucking him wouldn't be any different than with anyone else.

Her gaze lowered to his throat. She wasn't any good at sex, and as soon as he realized that, he would excuse himself and leave. It would feel good while he pumped his dick inside her, but it wouldn't be enough to make her come. And the shame when he left her would leave her hollow.

"What's wrong, little bird?" His brows furrowed, and he put a hand on her cheek, using his thumb under her chin to tip her head back until she was forced to meet his gaze. "I won't push you into anything you don't want. But I'm not going to lie and tell you I don't want you. Because I do, and I have since the first time I laid eyes on you."

All she could do was stare at him with wide unblinking eyes. So, he had noticed her as well, just like she had noticed him. Did that mean he was as drawn to her as she was to him, or was she just a new potential hookup? All the other women in their group were mated, so it wasn't like there were a lot of choices when it came to bed partners at the moment.

His eyes dipped to her lips, and she automatically licked them. Letting him fuck her might be a bad idea, but that didn't mean they couldn't kiss. In fact they needed the practice if they were going to pull this off. He hadn't been wrong to suggest they talk, but actions were what would convince Amber of how they felt about each other.

Lifting up on her toes, she threw her arms around his neck and crushed her lips to his.

He froze, clearly taken off guard, but it didn't last more than a second. Then his arms came around her and pressed her tightly against his body. Tilting his head a little to the side, he parted his lips and thrust his tongue into her mouth.

Nes moaned as much from his dominance of her mouth as from his delicious taste. Did he taste this amazing the last time their lips met? And if so, why didn't she remember?

Rubbing her tongue along his, she squirmed against his hard body. She wanted to peel his clothes off and feel his skin slide against her own. Glorious images of him naked and pleasuring himself assailed her, and moisture pooled between her legs.

His hands cupped her ass and pulled her closer, and she gasped into his mouth when his hard cock pressed against her clit.

"Wrap your legs around my waist, little bird."

His words were mumbled against her lips, but they felt almost like a command she couldn't disobey. She needed to do as he asked, and when he lifted her, she didn't hesitate.

A long moan was drawn from her when she tightened her legs around him. His erection was hard against her pussy, making her clit throb with anticipation.

Gawen turned them around and took a few steps, the thick ridge in his pants rubbing her bundle of nerves with each one. Then, her back hit the wall, and his hips started rocking against her with purpose.

She tore her lips from his. "Gawen." His name was little more than an elaborate gasp.

"Yes, little bird." His blue eyes glowed like they were lit from within. "What do you want? Tell me."

"Just…more." She swallowed hard, her breaths coming in gasps. The friction felt so good. It might not be enough to make her come, but even if she didn't, it would be worth it. Feeling Gawen's erection and having all his attention focused on her was intoxicating.

"Like this?" He rubbed harder against her, using longer strokes. "Be specific, little bird. I want to see you fall apart."

A trickle of ice rushed down her spine, and she froze. "That's not necessary."

His movements immediately stopped, and his eyes narrowed as they drilled into hers. "What do you mean it's not necessary?"

"I…" She squeezed her eyes shut against his

probing stare. "You can finish without me. It's fine. I don't mind."

She jerked in surprise when he brushed a soft kiss against her closed eyelid. "But I mind, Nes. I don't care if I come as long as I get to hear you cry out in pleasure."

Her eyes popped open in surprise at his tender response. "But I can't. No one has ever been able to—"

Nes bit her lip to stop herself when she realized what she was saying. She hadn't meant to tell him that. It wasn't his problem. He wasn't with her because he loved her. This was all pretend.

His eyes were warm with more than desire when he gave her a small smile. "Will you allow me to try? You can tell me to stop at any time, and I will. But I'd love the opportunity to make you come."

Nes's heart was racing in her chest. How could she let him try when failure would gut her? Sex had been a disappointment for her with every man she'd been with, but those men hadn't really mattered. They hadn't been special. And they hadn't really tried.

But Gawen was special. He was important to her, even after such a short time. And there was something in his eyes that told her he wouldn't give up so easily. But would it be enough? Because if it wasn't, watching the pity in his eyes when he walked away would tear her heart out.

This is a mistake, a huge mistake. But what if it's not? After pulling in a shaky breath, she made her decision and nodded. "Okay."

A huge grin spread across Gawen's face. "Thank you. I'll make sure you won't regret it."

Her legs were still wrapped around his waist when he turned and carried her to the bed. Putting a knee on the mattress, he lowered her gently down onto her back.

His hands moved to the button of her jeans, where he paused and lifted his gaze to hers. Staring into her eyes with a small smile on his face, he slowly undid her pants. "Breathe, little bird. I've got you."

She hadn't even realized she'd been holding her breath. Letting it go in a whoosh of air, she closed her eyes as embarrassment heated her face. What did he think of her? He was acting all gentle and caring, while she was acting like an inexperienced and awkward teenager. How long would it take for him to understand that she had no idea what she was doing in the bedroom and walk away laughing?

"Come back to me, Nes. I won't continue until you open your eyes and look at me. And if you don't want me to keep going, that's fine too." His large hands cupped her cheeks.

She opened her eyes slowly until she stared up into his. They were dark with worry, creases marring his beautiful features. "I'm sorry." The words were no more than a low whisper passing over her lips.

His eyes narrowed and anger suddenly replaced the concern from a second ago. "What do you mean you're sorry?"

Nes's lungs seized in her chest, and she pushed her head back against the mattress to create distance between them. Hunching her shoulders, she brought her arms up to cover her chest. Panic was rising like a tidal wave inside her, telling her to run, but her sanity was still present enough for her to know that she wouldn't be able to get far if she tried.

Gawen's eyes widened. All traces of his anger drained from his face in an instant. His hands vanished from her face as he straightened and took a step back. "You're scared of me."

He ran a hand through his hair while he studied her face. "I'm so sorry. I'm not angry with you but with whoever hurt you. Please tell me who it was so I can punish them for what they did to you." He seemed calm, but the muscle ticking in his jaw spoke of his simmering rage.

CHAPTER 19

Nes

Nes pulled in a shaky breath while she considered his words. She believed him that his anger hadn't been directed at her, but her body was still trembling with fear.

What had just happened? Why had she reacted like that? She couldn't remember ever having reacted like that before. Anger hadn't scared her before, so why now? And with the man she wanted more than she had ever wanted anyone.

Gawen let out a deep sigh, and she realized he was still waiting for her to say something.

"I…" She paused, searching for a plausible explanation, but when his eyebrows rose in expectation, she decided to tell him the truth. Whatever the truth was. "I'm not sure why I reacted like that. No one has hurt—"

Images assailed her, and she gasped, sudden terror

like a sharp claw fastening around her neck and sinking into her flesh.

"*You know you want this before you go,*" John had said while palming his hard dick.

She had started to shake her head, getting ready to leave after spending an awkward night with him at his place. They had already had sex a couple of times, both with him telling her how he was the best she'd ever had and making her feel like shit for not really enjoying it.

"*Of course you do.*" He had smirked and grabbed her upper arms before walking her backward until her back hit the wall.

She had let him because she didn't want to get into a fight with him. Her focus had been on finding a way to refuse him without having to use her strength to overpower him, but it had been a mistake.

He had surprised her with his sudden speed and aggressiveness. Before she had realized what he intended, she had been face down on the bed with her panties around her knees and his dick pushing into her.

And she had done nothing to stop him. The shock had left her numb, and she hadn't been able to do anything while he used her for his own pleasure. It hadn't lasted for more than a few minutes, and she had avoided him ever since, but the incident must have left a deeper scar in her mind than she had thought.

"Nes." Gawen's voice seemed to come from far away.

She blinked to regain her focus. The whole episode with John had been humiliating, and she still hadn't been able to come to terms with the fact that she didn't stop it. She, a shifter, hadn't been able to stop a human from doing whatever he wanted with her. And she didn't feel like revealing that fact to Gawen and destroying his opinion of her.

"Please talk to me, Nes." His eyes were filled with worry and something like despair when she met his gaze. "I know someone hurt you. Please let me help you."

Biting her lower lip, she silently debated what to tell him. He had made no secret of the fact that she turned him on, but he had treated her with respect from the moment they met and never pushed her to do anything she didn't want to. And she couldn't imagine he ever would. The way he had spoken earlier, it was clear that her pleasure was important to him. He didn't want to use her just to get off.

Nes took a deep breath to steady her voice before she spoke. "I had a bad experience, that's all. Nothing serious." After pushing up on her elbows, she swung her legs off the bed and sat up.

"I don't agree." He frowned before turning and sitting down next to her, leaving a few inches between their thighs. "That kind of reaction doesn't come from nothing. Do you mind telling me what happened?" His hands tightened into fists in his lap like he was steeling himself for whatever she was going to say.

Yes, I mind. Nes fisted her hand in the sheets beside her where he couldn't see. She had the overpowering urge to tell him no and leave the room to make sure he didn't ask her any more questions. But what if he turned around and told her brother what had happened? Henry would stop at nothing to extract the truth from her, and he would go after John even if she begged him not to. "Fine. But you'll have to promise me not to tell my brother."

His lips tightened into a hard line before he let out a deep sigh. "Okay, if that's what it takes for you to tell me. But I want to know everything." His features might as well have been carved in granite for how rigid they were.

Shit! She had counted on being able to tell him just enough to stop his questions, but she had a feeling he would know it if she left something out.

His hand covered hers, startling her, and when she didn't pull her hand away, he braided his fingers with hers and held on. "Let me help you, Nes." His blue eyes filled with warmth. "I might only be your pretend lover, but I care about you."

"You care about me?" She couldn't keep the doubt out of her voice. "Why? You don't even know me."

He shrugged. "Perhaps, but I like you. And I'd like to get to know you. Now, tell me who I need to kill."

She blanched and yanked her hand away from his. "No, you can't."

"I'm joking." He raked his fingers through his hair. "Sort of."

Nes shook her head as she took in the anger in his eyes. "I can't let you kill anyone. Besides, he doesn't deserve that. It was mostly my own fault."

His eyes narrowed on her like he didn't believe her. "He? What did he do to you that was mostly your fault?" His voice had dropped an octave and filled with gravel, clearly not believing her.

This isn't a good idea. She gripped the sheet tighter in her hand. "I don't think I feel comfortable telling you. It's in the past and nothing can be done to change it anyway."

"Fine." He rose and stalked toward the door. "You can tell your brother then."

"No!" After jumping to her feet, she raced after him and just managed to squeeze herself between him and the door in time to prevent him from opening it. "Please don't tell him. I don't want him to be disappointed in me."

Gawen stopped and frowned down at her. "How can he be disappointed that someone hurt you? That doesn't make sense."

Staring up at him, she silently berated herself for speaking without thinking. The hole she had started digging for herself was getting bigger by the minute. If she wasn't careful, she would end up getting a man killed for being an idiot and expecting her to go along with whatever he wanted.

"I..." Tears suddenly filled her eyes, and she looked down to avoid Gawen seeing her weakness. She had wished she wasn't a shifter so many times because she didn't want a mate, but beneath that was the simple truth that she wasn't strong enough and brave enough to call herself a wolf. She didn't fit in, and hiding among humans had been her way of avoiding her parents' and their pack's expectations and judgment.

Gawen's hands smoothed slowly up her arms before he wrapped his arms around her and pulled her close.

She let herself rest against his tall strong form, tucking her head beneath his chin and taking a deep breath to stave off the tears running down her cheeks and coating his warm skin. It was wrong to give in to her weakness and rely on someone else to hold her up, but she couldn't muster the strength to fight it at the moment. She felt so bone tired, like she had been swimming against the tide for years without rest.

"You're strong, Nes. Much stronger than you think." Gawen's deep voice was soft and soothing as he rested his chin on her head. "But no one can be strong all the time. That's impossible. We all need someone to help us through the hard times, and it's a show of strength to seek that help."

Nes let his words sink in. It was almost like he knew exactly how she was feeling and what she needed to hear. He had magic and could heal physical wounds, but perhaps his magic could heal emotional ones as well. Or maybe it wasn't magic but just a part of who he was.

Wrapping her arms around his waist, she swallowed down the lump that had lodged in her throat. "Thank you. I think I needed to hear that right now."

A large hand caressed the length of her spine before curving around her nape. Warmth sank into her skin, and she suddenly felt lighter, like all her worries were lifted off her shoulders. "What are you doing? Are you using your magic on me to make me feel better?"

"I..." He paused and she could hear the confusion in his voice. "Does this make you feel better?"

"Yes." She nodded, her cheek rubbing against the base of his throat. "It's like you're draining away everything that's been bothering me for the last few months. Was that your intention?"

CHAPTER 20

Gawen

Gawen's eyes widened when he realized she was right. He had been using his magic on her without even thinking about it, and not to heal a physical wound but the pain she was suffering because of whatever had happened to her. And it seemed to help her. Was this one of the new powers Aidan had mentioned that might develop over time? Or had he already possessed it this whole time without even knowing it?

"To be honest I didn't even know I could do that." He chuckled as joy spread through him at the knowledge that he was helping Nes feel better. "But I'm happy it's helping you. That's all I want. I'd still like you to tell me what happened, though. Someone hurt you, and I don't want anything like that to happen again."

She turned her head, her lips brushing over his skin, causing a spark of heat to shoot through his body directly to his deflated cock. "Thank you for saying that, but you're not going to be there all the time to protect me."

But I want to be. He clamped his mouth shut to stop himself from telling her exactly that. It would come across as controlling and possessive, and he had no right to be either of those things with her. "But I'm here right now, so let me help you while I can."

Her hand fisted the back of his shirt. "That's—"

A sharp knock on the door made them both jerk in surprise.

"Gawen?" Henry's voice sounded through the door, and Nes jerked for a second time in his arms.

"Yes, just give us a minute." Scowling at the door, Gawen couldn't help inwardly cursing Henry for bothering them. Another few minutes and Nes might have confided in him, but now he would have to put that on hold and find a way to persuade her to open up to him later. And who knew when there would be time for that.

Reluctantly letting go of the beautiful woman in his arms, he took a step back.

She swiped at her tear-soaked cheeks before lifting her gaze to his and giving him a small smile. "Thank you." Before he could say anything, she shot past him and into the bathroom.

"Damn you, Henry," he grumbled beneath his breath before he let out a frustrated sigh and opened the door just enough to meet the man's gaze.

Nes's brother studied Gawen's face for a second before his gaze dropped to Gawen's chest, and he grinned. "Not a trace. You really have superior healing compared to the rest of us. How are you feeling?"

"Better." But he couldn't find it in him to return his alpha's smile.

"Good." Henry took a step to the side and tried to look beyond him into the room, probably looking for his sister.

Gawen pressed his lips together to avoid ordering his alpha to leave them alone. All he wanted was a little more time alone with Nes. But that wasn't going to happen. Opening the door wide, he took a step to the side to let Henry get a good view of the entire room.

"Where's Nes?" Henry's gaze swung around the room before settling on Gawen.

As if on cue, the bathroom door opened, and Nes stepped out, wearing a calm smile like she hadn't been crying just a minute ago. "Brother, are you checking up on me?"

"No." Henry gave his sister a warm smile before swinging his gaze back to Gawen with a considering expression on his face. "I'm here to ask Gawen if he's ready to—"

"No, he's not."

Gawen's eyes widened at Nes's sharp tone and the lick of her power that heated his skin. He'd been about to say yes, but he found himself keeping his mouth shut and waiting to see how Henry would respond.

The alpha frowned at his sister before turning to look at Gawen with an eyebrow raised in question. "Is that true? Aidan is getting impatient, but I think the others would rather be sure that you're completely healed before you try again. Nobody wants a repeat of what happened before."

"And neither do I." Gawen shot Nes a glance, taking in her stern expression and her arms crossed over her chest. Just minutes ago she had told him he couldn't protect her, but here she was trying to protect him.

A grin spread across his face when he met Henry's gaze. "But I think I'm ready to try again if your sister will let me."

"I won't." Nes's fingers dug into his bicep. "At least not yet. Tell Aidan he'll have to wait another half hour."

Gawen shrugged while secretly relishing Nes's protectiveness. "You heard the lady." He had no idea why this woman thought she was weak, when her strength was so evident to him. But he was going to find out. If only she would trust him enough to tell him what that asshole did to her.

Henry's laughter took him by surprise, and Nes snatched her hand back like she had just been burned. "I guess I'll see you downstairs in half an hour then." The red-haired man spun and disappeared down the hallway without waiting for confirmation.

Gawen closed the door before turning to look at Nes. But she was standing with her back to him, and the only indication he had of what she was thinking was the tension in her shoulders.

He wanted her to talk to him, but his attempts at persuading her had failed, and he had a feeling pushing her any further would only make her resent him. But perhaps there was another way.

After crossing the floor to the bed, he lay down on his back. "Okay, I'm resting. I assume that's what you want me to do for the next half hour?" Instead of looking at her, he closed his eyes and rested the back of one hand over his eyes trying not to smile.

Several seconds went by in silence. Then the bed moved as Nes settled beside him without touching him. "Yes. It's safer for everyone if you're fully healed and rested before you attempt whatever you were doing before. I don't want to see you hurt again. Or anyone else for that matter."

"Fair enough. How are you feeling? Are you still feeling better, or did my magic only give you some temporary relief?" He hoped it would have a lasting effect, but he had no way of knowing until he gained some experience with his new ability.

"I'm better but..."

He frowned at her hesitation. "But what?"

She blew out a breath. "I can't stand the thought of you getting hurt again. What if next time it's worse? What if you're..."

He removed his hand covering his eyes and turned to look at her. Her eyes were dark with worry.

Her concern for him made his chest swell with an emotion he didn't want to name. It was too soon and probably unwelcomed if he was to show it. She might worry about him, but that didn't have to mean anything other than that she considered him a friend.

"I won't die, Nes." Giving her a warm smile to reassure her, he rolled onto his side. "And you've already seen how fast I heal. Now turn onto your side." He indicated for her to face away from him.

After studying his face for a second, she did as he asked before scooting back until she was flush against his chest.

His smile widened. She might not see a future with him, but he was still lucky to have this time with her. Only that morning he had thought he might not see her again, or at least not for a long time. But his alpha had had other plans. He realized Henry had been thinking about his sister's safety and not Gawen's infatuation with her, but the end result had been the same. They were here together.

Nes's soft body was pressed against his, and it was impossible not to react to her closeness. His cock swelled in the hopes of finally getting some action, but that would have to wait.

This was the perfect opportunity to give her what he had promised her earlier—if she would let him. But judging from the way she had eagerly closed the distance between them, he had a feeling she might.

Nestling into the crook of her neck, he kissed her soft skin in the dip above her collarbone. She let out a small gasp, and he took that as an invitation to kiss his way up to her ear before biting down gently on her lobe.

"Gawen," she moaned and squirmed against him, her ass rubbing against his rigid shaft.

A shudder of need racked his body, but he mentally shook it off. This was his opportunity to focus on Nes and her pleasure, and he couldn't let his own desire get in the way of that.

He put a hand on her hip before smoothing it up her side beneath her shirt. All the while kissing and nibbling along her shoulder and neck.

Nes tipped her head back against his shoulder, giving him better access to her neck. It was a clear sign that she was enjoying what he was doing to her and didn't want him to stop, but he had no intention of going any further without her expressed permission.

"I want to touch you, little bird. Everywhere.

Would you like that?"

"Yes. Please." Her voice was breathy. "I want your hands on me."

And my mouth, I hope. He grinned against the skin of her neck. Her scent of vanilla and raspberries was already driving him crazy, and her taste would probably be just as intoxicating.

He sat up and unclasped her bra with one hand. "Sit up. I need full access to your beautiful body to be able to touch you the way you deserve."

She did as he told her without turning to look at him, and he quickly removed her shirt and bra. A blush crept up her neck and into her face, but she didn't pull away or tell him to stop.

When he had first met her the day before, she had seemed so confident. But he was quickly coming to realize it was all an act, probably as a result of some asshole's mistreatment. It made him want to strangle the jerk slowly for whatever he had done to her, and he might end up doing just that if he ever found out who the fucker was.

Taking a deep breath, Gawen pushed his plans for revenge to the back of his mind. He had a beautiful female wolf in his arms who needed a demonstration of how amazing she was and that she had nothing to fear from him. Everything else was insignificant compared to her pleasure and wellbeing.

He leaned in and kissed her nape. With her short spiky hair, there were no long locks covering up her slender neck, and he found he preferred it.

Reaching around her, he brushed his thumb along the underside of her breast. "I'd like you to take off your pants while I rearrange the pillows. Then I want you to sit between my legs with your back resting against my chest. How does that sound?"

"Good." She nodded as she moved off the bed. "But what about you? Aren't you going to undress?"

"No."

Her head snapped around to look at him, confusion creasing her brows. "But—"

"I'll take off my damaged shirt but not my pants." Gawen winked at her. "Next time, though, if you want, I'll be naked and ready for whatever you want to do to me."

CHAPTER 21

Nes

Nes studied his face while she pushed her pants and panties down her thighs. When he had said he wanted to touch her everywhere she had assumed he was going to fill her with his cock, but apparently that wasn't what he had meant.

His gaze dropped to her bare pussy, and he groaned. But his gaze didn't linger. Instead, he tore off his shirt before arranging the plump pillows against the headboard.

She let out a silent sigh. What did he really mean when he said he wanted to touch her everywhere? If he was planning some kind of innocent massage she was probably going to spontaneously combust. She might not come even if he gave it his best to make that happen, but she still wanted him to at least try.

"Come here, little bird." Gawen was resting against the pillows with his legs splayed and one corner of his lips lifted in a sexy smile. He patted the bed between his legs. "We've only got about twenty minutes, and I want to hear you moan my name before our time is up."

So, everywhere wasn't merely an innocent massage then. Her heart rate sped up at the thought of what he promised to do to her. Would he be able to do it? Would he become the first man who gave her an orgasm? She sincerely hoped so. They might never end up together, but at least she would have a unique memory of their time together.

Crawling on her hands and knees across the bed toward him, she enjoyed the way his heated gaze lingered first on her breasts and then on her face.

His hand palmed his cock, and she felt her eyes widen when she noticed the massive bulge threatening to tear the fabric of his jeans. It looked uncomfortable, and instead of turning around and sitting down like he had requested, she reached out toward the button of his jeans to free the monster.

"No." His fingers wrapped around her wrist. "If you touch me now, I won't be able to keep my promise to you, and I never break a promise."

She frowned as she kept staring at his rigid shaft. "But isn't it uncomfortable?"

"A little, but I can handle it as long as I get to touch you."

She snorted as she lifted her gaze to his. "Are you sure? You do realize I'm going to squash that thing when I lean against your chest, right?"

He chuckled. "I'll be fine. If you can handle my cock poking into your back, I can handle you leaning against me."

Nes wanted to argue that her back was less sensitive than his dick, but perhaps it was better to let him experience that firsthand. It might persuade him to take his pants off, and she wouldn't mind that at all. Just the thought of touching him was enough to make her channel clench and remind her how empty it was. She had always enjoyed the feeling of being filled, even if it had never been enough to make her climax.

After turning around, she sat down between Gawen's legs. Leaning back carefully, she waited for him to change his mind and stop her. But he never did. His hard length dug into her back when she let herself rest against him, but he didn't complain or push her away.

"Are you ready to let me explore your body and make you feel good?"

His voice in her ear was deeper than before, and a small moan escaped her when her clit took notice and more moisture gathered between her legs. She wasn't sure she had ever been this wet for anyone, and he hadn't even touched her yet. "Yes."

"Then relax." He put a hand on her forehead and gently pulled her back until her head was resting against his muscular shoulder.

No sooner had she settled against him than his hand cupped her right breast, and she sucked in a surprised breath. His large hand kneaded her flesh before he pinched her nipple, sending a spark of pleasure to her clit.

Pressing her thighs together, she bit her lip against the need to touch herself. She had tried that once with the first man she'd had sex with, but apparently that was unacceptable. He had taken it as a sign that she found his performance lacking and made an excuse to leave as soon as he had come inside her. Needless to say, she'd never made that mistake again, and she most certainly wasn't going to make it with Gawen.

His other hand came up to caress her left breast, and she automatically arched her back to push into his heavenly touch. His movements were sure and languid, not rushed like he was impatient to get to the next step of fucking her.

He kissed her cheek before nibbling along her jaw until he reached the corner of her mouth. "Kiss me, Nes. I need your mouth."

Smiling, she turned her head, about to ask him where he wanted it. But before she could utter a word, his mouth covered hers, and his tongue swiped inside her mouth.

All thoughts seized, and her focus narrowed down to how he made her feel. His tongue stroked and caressed, stoking the heat that was building in her lower belly. And his hands were still on her breasts, playing with her sensitive nipples and making her squirm against him and rub her thighs together in an effort to get some much-needed relief for her throbbing clit.

"Spread your legs for me, little bird." He mumbled the words against her lips, and it took her a second to understand what he was saying.

Her eyes popped open, and she stared up at him, struggling to focus with his face so close to hers.

He pulled his head back a little and gave her a toothy grin. "Please. I can't touch you if you don't allow me access."

A mixture of anticipation and trepidation raced

down her spine as she let her thighs fall open. She was desperate for his touch down there, but she didn't want to disappoint him when she couldn't climax.

His gaze landed on her pussy, and her whole body tensed. She didn't know what to expect from him. He had already made this into the most memorable experience she had ever had in bed with a man, but the next couple of minutes would either enhance or destroy it.

He let go of her right breast before caressing slowly down her stomach. Holding her breath, she stared at his large hand approaching her most sensitive area. His fingers were longer and thicker than a typical man's. Would that make a difference to how it would feel when he touched her?

She gasped when one long digit slid through her slick folds.

"Fuck," Gawen rasped next to her ear. "You're so wet for me. It almost makes me regret using my fingers instead of filling you with my cock."

Putting her hands on his thighs, she tried to sit up. "But we can—"

"No!" His arm wrapped around her torso under her breasts and held her locked against him. He took a deep breath, like he was struggling to maintain control. "I want to make you come. Besides, I've got a feeling that one time won't be enough with you, and we don't have time for a sex marathon right now."

CHAPTER 22

Nes

Nes was stunned silent. Sex marathon. That sounded amazing and exactly like something she wanted. Just the thought of having him pump into her for more than a couple of minutes made her pussy clench with longing.

The finger that had been playing along her slit suddenly dipped inside her, drawing a surprised moan from her. But it turned to a whimper when he pulled it out again almost immediately. She wanted to yell at him to put it back, but she knew better than to voice what she wanted. All it would earn her was anger or possibly ridicule. Although that might not be true with Gawen. He was different from the men she'd been with, and perhaps she shouldn't judge him by how other men had treated her.

She was just trying to gather the necessary courage to tell Gawen to slide his finger back inside her when he did something unexpected. Pressing her head back against his shoulder, she let out a surprised yell when his finger slid over her clit. And she soon realized it wasn't an accident when the pad of his finger continued gliding fore and back over her swollen nub like he knew exactly what that did to her.

"I think you like that." His dark voice was filled with a wide smile. "Then perhaps you'll like this as well."

His arm around her torso disappeared and before she realized what he intended, a long digit delved into her depths, and she just about bucked off the bed.

"Gawen, what are you... Oh, Gawen." His finger slid over that sensitive area inside her again and again while he rubbed her clit. Heat built in her lower belly, and she tipped her pelvis forward in her desperation to come.

"You're so beautiful." His voice was like a purr vibrating against her ear. "I'm so lucky to be here with you and see you like this. It's time for you to reach for the pleasure you want and take it."

Heat was swirling inside her, but no matter how much she reached for the orgasm she so desperately wanted it stayed just out of her grasp. All her muscles were straining, and her breathing was no more than shallow gasps.

And then he stopped.

"No!" The word echoed in the room as she turned her head to look at him. This wasn't how this was supposed to end. Not with him. She had been so close, and with what he had been doing to her, she'd actually thought she would climax.

His glowing blue eyes met hers, and there was a

gentle smile on his lips. "You need to relax and breathe. You're trying to force it, but it won't happen like that. This isn't a competition or a performance, Nes."

She blinked at him before taking a deep breath and letting it out along with the tension in her muscles.

"Good girl." His smile widened. "Now let me do my job while you close your eyes and just feel."

His fingers started moving again, but slower this time like he wanted to make sure she didn't tense up again.

Closing her eyes, she marveled at the deftness of his fingers. He knew exactly what he was doing, and he seemed to enjoy it.

Then, he added another digit inside her, and she moaned at the sense of fullness it created. It added depth to the pleasure building, and she couldn't help it when her hips started rocking to meet the fingers pumping into her.

She shuddered when he brushed his lips over her closed eyelid, before kissing his way down her cheek to the corner of her mouth all the while mumbling sweet nothings against her skin. "You're doing so well. Just feel and enjoy. This is not a race. I'm so lucky to be allowed to see you like this. To be able to play with your beautiful body. Just let go, little bird. Relax and let yourself fly."

The orgasm took her completely by surprise. One second she was basking in his sweet words, and the next she was soaring above the clouds on the crest of a tidal wave of pleasure.

He didn't let go of her but kept manipulating her body until the final shred of ecstasy faded, and she sagged against him, gasping for breath.

"Thank you," she mumbled, unable to peel her eyes open. Exhaustion was threatening to overpower her and pull her into a deep sleep, but she was fighting to stay awake, not ready to let go of her time with Gawen yet.

He chuckled, the sound ragged with what she could only assume was desire. "Any time, little bird. But next time I will be inside you when you come like that." His voice was gravelly, and the hard ridge digging into her back seemed to be even harder than it had been before.

There was a knock on the door, and she probably would have jerked at the intrusive sound if she'd had the energy.

"Our time's up," Gawen whispered close to her ear before he continued in a loud voice. "I'll be right there."

"Good. We're waiting." Aidan's voice sounded through the door.

"I wish I didn't have to leave you right now." Strong arms wrapped around her, and soft lips pressed a kiss to her temple. He gently moved her limp body until she was lying on her side on the mattress with her head resting on a soft pillow.

"Why don't you take a nap, and I'll be back before you know it." He tucked the crisp sheet around her before giving her another gentle kiss, and the next thing she knew, the door closed behind him, and she was alone.

She pulled in a deep breath and rolled slowly onto her back. Her body felt like it weighed a ton, and just the thought of lifting an arm was enough to make her groan.

It took effort to force her eyes open, and she blinked against the sharp light from the windows that made her want to close them again immediately. If she didn't know better, she would have thought someone had drugged her. But realistically she was probably just having a delayed reaction to everything that had happened in the last couple of days.

She had learned that there was such a thing as witches in the world, and one of them was trying to kill all shifters. Her brother had died at the hands of an evil witch, only to come back to life because he was bonded to a vampire who was also his true mate. Her parents' mating bond had been severed, and her mother had left the pack to pursue another life. And Nes had met the man of her dreams, and he had just given her a taste of what love could be like with the right man. It was a lot to take in, particularly when she'd barely gotten an hour's sleep the night before.

But there was no way she could stay in bed sleeping when Gawen was outside using magic that could literally blow up in his face. There was nothing she could do to prevent him from getting hurt, but she needed to be present and ready if it happened again.

After flinging off the sheet, she rolled out of bed, almost tumbling to the floor before she could find her footing. She stumbled around, gathering her clothes off the floor before making her way to the bathroom.

Gawen might already be outside, and she needed to be as close to him as possible without distracting him. But she also needed to be alert.

After turning on the shower, she twisted the knob to cold. It wouldn't be pleasant, but at least she would be awake and clean by the end of it.

CHAPTER 23

Gawen

Gawen pulled in a deep breath as he took in the three mates staring at him with expressions ranging from hostile to stern. He had no trouble understanding why. Leith, Michael, and Bryson were all concerned about their mates' safety after what had happened when Gawen lost focus earlier.

But he felt better now. Knowing that he had given Nes something no one else had given her before had somehow settled him. She might not choose him as a boyfriend or mate, but at least he had given her a positive experience. And hopefully, it had proven to her how amazing and valuable she was. Because she was much more sensitive and vulnerable than he had thought when he first met her. It didn't mean she was weak, though.

His little bird had unraveled so beautifully in his arms. His still-hard cock, hidden by the clean shirt he had put on before leaving the room, was evidence of that.

Gawen had planned to taste her, but he had quickly realized he wouldn't be able to give her the sole focus she needed if he put his mouth on her. He had been too wound up as it was and barely hanging on to a thread of his sanity by the time she came.

"Are you all ready?" Aidan's question addressed all four of them, but the man's eyes were on Gawen.

"Yes." He met Aidan's gaze and gave the man a firm nod.

Another three confirmative answers sounded from around them.

"Good." Aidan looked at each of them in turn. "Let's continue where we left off last time. I want to see an A on that rock over there." He pointed in the direction of the rock without looking at it.

Gawen let his magic swirl inside him before he blended it with the others, carefully melding it together to create a power as uniform as possible.

He let Aidan take the lead, directing their power toward the rock while Gawen focused on tightening their combined magic into a potent ball of energy.

Dust exploded from the rock and blocked their view when they hit it, but they didn't need to see the rock to complete the task. They kept going until they had completed the movements necessary to form the letter A.

As soon as the dust settled to reveal the crooked but unmistakable letter, cheers and sounds of approval rose from the people present.

A female voice drew his attention to the person who had come to stand next to Bryson. Nes. She had come outside after all, and when she smiled at him, a mix of pride and concern made his heart speed up.

Gawen loved that she had come to watch. Having her within his line of sight was comforting, but it also put her at risk if something went wrong. He didn't know which he wanted more, to take her in his arms and kiss her or order her to go back inside.

"I think we're ready." Aidan's words pulled Gawen's attention away from Nes and back to the enforcer. "We've all had our experiences with Amber, some more violent and traumatizing than others. I want you all to take your experience with her and use it in our search for her. This might have started as an unattainable idea, but I've since come to realize that all great ideas tend to start like that. This group has a wide range of abilities and a tremendous amount of combined power. What at first sounded impossible might very well be possible for us." He paused like he wanted his words to sink in.

Gawen nodded more as a confirmation that he had heard Aidan's words than that he actually believed them. But he was the one who had first voiced the idea, so he couldn't very well back out now. It was worth a try in any case. And if it didn't work, which it most likely wouldn't, they would just have to come up with some other way to find the witch and attract her attention.

But there was also a chance they wouldn't have to. Based on how she kept coming back to attack these people or someone close to them, Amber might already be on her way to kill them all.

"I would like Sabrina to take the lead on this one." The enforcer smiled at the blond witch standing next to him. "You are the one who has the ability to find people."

Sabrina frowned. "Amber seems to know how to block me, though, so it's unlikely that I'll be able to locate her. But I'll do my best."

"And that's all I'm asking of you." Aidan smiled. "The rest of us will support you with our power and help you search."

Gawen let his power flow and meld with the others as before. But this time instead of the power staying close like a tight ball, Sabrina sent it out like a sheer veil to cover a vast area. She was looking for the unique energy signature belonging to Amber.

The veil stretched and moved, touching masses of people on its way. It was incredible to witness another magic user's ability in practice like this. Like an open window to a part of another person's mind. He didn't know why he was able to see this so clearly when he hadn't with Aidan, but it might have something to do with Aidan being an enforcer, or perhaps that the man was much more powerful than the rest of them.

Gawen wasn't sure how much time had gone by when Sabrina reeled the veil back in and let her power fade. The rest of them pulled back their magic as well.

"Well, that didn't work as I'd liked. Although, I'm not surprised." Sabrina let out a disappointed sigh. "But I'd hoped to at least get a general indication of her whereabouts."

Aidan smiled. "Don't worry. We're not done yet. There's something else we can—"

A searing pain stabbed through Gawen's head, like someone had just run a sword through him. But it wasn't a physical object that had penetrated his skull.

The feel of the magic was familiar, and he immediately realized who was responsible for the excruciating pain.

Blinding rage surged through him, making him gasp with its intensity. But it wasn't his rage.

I'm done being pursued. No more. From now on I'm the one who calls the shots. Amber's words rang through his head so loud he gasped with the stab of each syllable. *Prepare to die. You've caused enough problems.*

His thoughts immediately went to Nes. There was no way he was going to let Amber hurt his little bird. He'd happily die protecting her if that was what it took.

I know where you are. You can't hide from me. I'm more powerful than all of you now. You won't be able to stop me anymore. There was a sick kind of glee coloring her tone.

Gawen didn't believe her, though. She might have grown in power, but her overconfidence had grown much faster. And that would be her downfall.

Fighting through the pain, he gathered his magic. Not all of it, but just enough to stall her attempt at taking over his mind completely.

You can't hurt us since you'll soon be dead. He pushed the words at her. *And I'll be the first to dance on your grave with my soon-to-be mate. I can't wait.*

CHAPTER 24

Gawen

A roar of fury filled Gawen's mind, and his whole body went rigid with the accompanying agony. But his magic kept her from taking over.

The pain vanished as fast as it had appeared. But it took him a few seconds to reconnect with his senses.

He was lying on his back on the ground, his clothes soaked from lying in the wet grass for the second time that day.

"Gawen." Nes's voice was filled with fear, and her scent was tainted by it as well. Her fingers were digging into his biceps as she leaned over him.

He opened his eyes to stare up into her dark-blue ones that were wide with terror. "I'm fine."

She didn't look like she believed him, the way her eyes roamed his face, searching for any sign that he wasn't. "What happened?"

"Amber." Her name left a sour taste in his mouth,

and his lips twisted with distaste. "She got into my head."

Nes's head snapped back like he had just hit her in the face. "No. How?" She swung her head around, scanning the garden and beyond. "She's here?"

"No." He shook his head.

"How can you be so sure? Do you know where she is?" Aidan's expression was tight with concern.

"Edinburgh or somewhere around there." Gawen pushed up on his arms until he was sitting in the wet grass. "I don't know precisely how I know that. I just do."

"I'll go tell Callum and Vamika. It will narrow down their search." Bryson, who had been standing by Gawen's feet, turned to leave.

"Then tell them she's on her way here to kill us."

Bryson snapped his head around to stare at him, but before he could say anything, Sabrina beat him to it.

"She spoke to you." It wasn't a question.

Gawen nodded. "She did and she was furious. Apparently, we have stepped on her toes a few too many times, and she's lost her patience with us. We don't have to try to find her. She'll come to us."

"We have some time to prepare. It will take her a few hours to get here from Edinburgh." Leith's body was practically radiating tension when he reached out and pulled his mate close to his side.

"Yes." Gawen turned to look at Nes, still kneeling by his side, and took her hand in his. "And there's a chance she'll come for us first. I told her we'd kill her, and my mate-to-be and I would be dancing on her grave. She might not be able to resist the possibility of more power, even though she bragged about being more powerful than us now."

Fear flashed in Nes's eyes for a second before they narrowed with anger. "Good. From what I've heard of her actions so far, she won't be able to resist the power she can gain from our mating. And we can use that to our advantage."

Gawen's heart swelled with hope when the words *our mating* rolled off her tongue like she meant them. God, he wanted that. And more than ever after having her unravel with pleasure in his arms. How he was ever going to be able to let her go after this was over, he had no idea. But hopefully, he wouldn't have to. The way she looked at him and acted around him had changed. Perhaps she was feeling what he was feeling, and it would make her reconsider her views on mating.

"I don't like that she can reach into someone's head from that far away. That's definitely new." Steph was standing with her arms crossed over her chest and a scowl on her face next to Michael. "And it proves that she wasn't just bragging about her power. Whether she's stronger than us or not is yet to be determined, but she's definitely stronger than she was before. And it probably means that she's killed again."

"And we're out of time." Michael's gaze was dark with worry when he looked at his mate. "This is going to be our last chance to defeat her. If we don't kill her now, she's going to kill us. And that's going to be the end of the world as we know it."

Leith nodded. "I believe you are right. It is now or never. I have never in my lifetime experienced anyone who has been able to increase their power like this. And fueled by revenge, that is a recipe for disaster."

Gawen rose, pulling Nes up with him while he held her gaze. "We need to come up with a plan. When she comes for us, we have to be ready. And I have an idea that I would like to discuss with you first. If you agree, we can share it with the others."

"Okay." Her lips parted as she studied his face like she was trying to guess what he was thinking.

He flashed her a smile before he looked at the people surrounding them. "Amber is smart. She might be angry, but she won't attack us without a well-thought-out plan. And she'll probably have a plan B and C as well just in case. She wants power but considering all the problems we've caused her, she might just decide to kill us outright without gaining anything other than less trouble. But we have to be prepared for both eventualities."

"We will be." Fia looked at Sabrina before she swung her gaze to Steph. "And the only way to do that is to come at her from different angles, both physically and magically. Our plan of attack has to be multifaceted, incorporating our various strengths and abilities. And I think we should make sure she attacks us close to the water."

Gawen's eyes widened in shock. Had Fia figured out what he was? Or was she thinking about Leith and Sabrina? The Loch Ness monster and his mermaid would certainly have an advantage in water, but Amber wouldn't be stupid enough to let herself be lured into the sea or a loch where she would clearly have a handicap.

Sabrina grinned. "I wouldn't mind drowning her, but I have a feeling it won't be as simple as that. She's not going to just wander into the sea at a whim, so if that's where we want her, we'll have to find a way to put her there."

Gawen breathed a silent sigh of relief. He didn't really know why he was holding on to his secret around these people, but just the thought of telling everyone what he was sent tremors of trepidation through his body. He would have to tell them at some stage, but he needed time to steel himself for the likely outcome before he could do it.

"Okay, we'll leave you to figure that out." Gawen nodded at Sabrina before tightening his grip on Nes's hand and leading her toward the house.

"It will be interesting to see what they come up with." There was a smile in Nes's voice. "But if we're going to be at a beach somewhere, we need to take that into account in our plans as well."

He nodded, suddenly unable to speak through the fear that tightened his chest. He was such an idiot. Taunting a powerful evil witch with the fact that he was soon-to-be mated. He had just painted a target on Nes's head. And it was too late to do anything about it.

There was only one thing that could stop Amber from focusing on Nes. To mate her before the witch arrived. But Nes would never agree to that, and he would never force her. Which meant he would have to protect her by staying at her side at all times.

CHAPTER 25

Nes

Nes let Gawen lead her up to their room. He had gone oddly quiet and rigid by her side, his hand so tight around hers it was almost painful. She didn't know what was bothering him, apart from the knowledge that they were about to be attacked by a cunning vindictive bitch, but she hoped he would tell her.

As soon as they entered the room, her eyes landed on the messy bed. Heat rose in her cheeks, and she quickly looked away to stop him from seeing her reaction. They had serious business to discuss and thinking about what Gawen's hands could do to her would distract her from the task.

A sharp tug on her hand sent her spinning directly into his arms, and her surprised squeak was silenced by his hungry mouth on hers. Heat raced through her, and she didn't hesitate to respond to his demanding kiss. It wasn't what she had expected when they had walked into the room, but she had absolutely no objections.

She wrapped her arms around his neck and held him tightly as their tongues twirled a wicked dance of desire. This was what she wanted to do, not fight a witch set on killing them all. All she wanted was some more time with Gawen to enjoy his talented fingers and a chance to repay him for what he had given her earlier.

"Fuck…Nes…I…need you." His lips were still on hers, his words barely understandable in between his kisses.

She believed him. His cock was like a steel bar poking into her belly. But there was a cure for his condition, one she would be happy to administer.

After pulling her head back, she smiled up at him. "I can help with that."

"You can?" His brows rose in surprise.

"Yes, of course." Chuckling, she reached between them to palm his hard cock. "I'd be happy to."

"Oh. Yes." There was a flicker of something that looked like disappointment before he gave her a wide grin. "But only if that's what you want."

She studied his face for a second, looking for any trace of the emotion she thought she'd seen. Had he meant something other than sexual desire when he said he needed her? A familiar shiver of anxiety raced down her spine, but she quickly pushed it away. There was no reason to believe that, particularly when looking into his glowing blue eyes.

Taking a step back, she grasped the hem of his shirt and pulled it over his head, revealing his superior upper body. The hard planes of his chest were right in front of her eyes and before she could think better of her impulse, she stepped into him and sucked his small nipple into her mouth.

He groaned and shuddered. "Fuck. That's—"

She pinned the small bud between her teeth, and he growled. The sound shot straight to her core and made her channel clench. But as much as she wanted him to touch her again, this wasn't about her.

Nes reached between them and snapped open the button of his jeans before letting go of his nipple and taking a step back. The anticipation of laying eyes on his hard length again was making her hot and wet.

She had wanted to touch him ever since she watched his dick jerk in his hand the night before at the farmhouse. And running the tip of her finger over him in the water of Loch Ness hadn't been nearly enough to satisfy that need.

Holding her breath, she carefully pulled down his zipper to reveal his straining shaft still covered by his boxer briefs. It was an enticing sight that only increased her eagerness to touch him.

Deciding to prolong her anticipation—and his— she pushed his jeans down his thighs while leaving his briefs in place. Getting down on her knees in front of him, she took her time easing his pants down his legs. It put her mouth within inches of his rigid cock.

Gawen's ragged breaths left no doubt that her actions were affecting him. And when she leaned forward and kissed the head of his dick through the fabric of his briefs, his abs tightened into a washboard so defined any bodybuilder would have been jealous. *Damn, this man is fine.*

"Little bird." His voice was low and sinful.

She lifted her gaze to his and was stunned by his blazing blue eyes and his gorgeous features made sharper by his obvious need. In the car she had thought he looked like an angel, but she had been wrong. This man was nothing short of a god.

"If you're aiming to make me lose my sanity, you're doing an excellent job of it." He reached down and cupped his balls. "If my nuts aren't blue by now it's a miracle. You've had me hard and in need of release probably a dozen times since this morning."

She couldn't help the laughter that burst from her. He was right and even though most of those times she hadn't meant to awaken his desire, there were a few when she had.

"Oh, you find that funny, do you?" His eyes narrowed, but his lips were curled in an amused smile.

"No, not really." She chuckled. "But then it kind of is. You're this amazing godlike creature, and I'm nothing but a regular shifter, not even a very feminine one at that. It's kind of hard to believe that I can turn you on like this."

His eyes were still narrow, but there was no longer a smile on his lips. "You are beautiful and feminine." His hands cupped her cheeks, gently pulling her up toward him as he stared into her eyes. "Don't ever let anyone tell you differently. You are the most stunning woman I have ever met, and if you were mine, I would make sure to show you that every day."

Nes didn't know what to say. The playfulness from a minute ago had changed into something completely different, and she didn't know what to believe. What was he trying to say? It almost sounded like he wanted something more than a pretend relationship with her.

And that should scare her, but instead it made her chest ache with a sudden longing to be his in every way.

He leaned down and slanted his lips over hers, gently licking her bottom lip until she touched the tip of her tongue to his. The kiss was slow and filled with so much more than lust. It was the best kiss she'd ever had, but it also made her shoulders tense with anxiety.

Nes wanted this man by her side and in her bed, not just this minute but for the foreseeable future. And if he had offered her that without the expectation of mating her, she might have said yes. But that wasn't going to happen. If he wanted her as much as it seemed, he wouldn't be satisfied just being her lover without a permanent commitment.

She broke their kiss slowly before pulling back and giving him a teasing smile. "Can I help you with that blue-balls problem now?"

His serious expression quickly changed into a wide grin, and the tension in her shoulders eased. "How can I possibly say no to that? I'm yours. You can do whatever you want to me."

Instead of saying anything, she kept her eyes on his as she sank to her knees in front of him. The muscles in his jaw tensed. When she put her hand on his hard abs, a shiver raced through his body.

She grasped the waistband of his boxer briefs and slowly pulled it away from his body until his hard cock sprang free. It rose proudly from between his legs, and from where she was sitting, it looked larger than it had appeared when she watched it dance in his hand. But that might have had something to do with the size of his hands compared to hers.

Wrapping her fingers around him, she relished the feel of his silky taut skin. His cock was beautiful. It was a term she had never considered using about a man's dick before, but Gawen's was.

"Oh fuck." His eyes lost focus for a second. "Do you mind if I sit down? I don't think I'm going to be able to stand through this."

"Of course." Smiling up at him, she followed him on her knees when he backed up toward the bed, all the while letting her hand gently caress his thick rod.

He sank down onto the bed with a groan. "This won't take long. I've craved the feeling of your hands on me ever since I met you yesterday."

"Only my hands?" She gave him a teasing grin, already knowing what the answer would be.

"Hell no." The hunger in his eyes made them sparkle like gemstones. "I could fuck you for a week straight, and it still wouldn't be enough."

Her jaw dropped, moisture soaking into her panties at the images he had just put in her head. Maybe she should take him up on that when they had gotten rid of Amber. To be fucked by this man for days, have him drive into her with abandon was…not something she should be considering.

She did the only thing she could do to distract herself from that utopian dream. Moving her hand down to the base of his thick shaft, she flattened her tongue against his hardness and slid it up until she caught the drops of precum leaking from the small slit at the tip.

"Little bird." The endearment sounded like a cross between a prayer and a curse. "You're going to be my destruction."

She chuckled as she stretched her lips over the head of his cock and sucked, forcing a long, deep growl from him. *I want to see you completely destroyed by my mouth, and I want to be the only one to do that to you ever again.*

The thought made her eyes go wide with panic, and she was grateful that she was leaning over his lap with her face hidden from his view. This man was threatening to ruin her resolve to stay unmated, and he didn't even seem to be trying. What would happen if he decided to pursue her? Would she be able to resist? And more importantly, would she want to?

Pushing the disturbing thoughts away, she focused on his swollen length and his pleasure. She wanted to give him this, even if it was only going to happen this once. He deserved it after what he had given her earlier.

Pushing her hand between his legs to massage his tight balls, she took as much of him as she could into her mouth.

"Fuck, fuck, fuck." He chanted the word as his fingers sank into her hair, and his thighs started vibrating with tension.

She swirled her tongue around the rim of his cockhead before flicking it against his frenulum, and he fisted his hands in her hair.

"Nes!" Her name erupted from his throat on a growl as hot cum shot down her throat. His power wrapped around her like a cocoon of love and lust, making her clit throb like she was already halfway to an orgasm.

CHAPTER 26

Gawen

Gawen forced himself to sit still while wave after wave of utter ecstasy crashed through him. His instinct told him to move, but he didn't want to choke her.

Her name lingered on his tongue after he had screamed it, and her sharp scent of arousal filled his nose and made him want to tear her clothes off, throw her on the bed, and bury himself inside her. But instead he let her wet mouth draw out his pleasure until his balls felt like they were running on empty.

"Stop. I can't take any more of your wicked mouth right now." He winced and tugged on her hair gently.

She let go of his still rigid shaft with a pop before tipping her head back and grinning up at him.

His heart clenched as he stared into her beautiful dark-blue eyes. He wanted her to be his forever, but unfortunately, he didn't think she felt the same about him. It had been disguised well, but she had avoided addressing his declaration earlier that he wanted her to be his.

You idiot. What did you think would happen? That she would fall into your arms and declare her undying love and devotion to you? He forced a smile to try to cover up the turmoil in his head, but apparently he wasn't very successful.

"What's wrong?" Nes cocked her head, and her brows pushed together. "You look...sad. Did I do something wrong?"

"No, not at all." He shook his head. "I don't think you could do anything wrong if you tried."

Her frown deepened. "Then what is it?"

"I can't help falling in love with you." The words were out of his mouth before he could stop them, but when he saw her face go pale, he wished he could take them back.

"That's..." She swallowed hard, her eyes blown wide and filled with near panic. "Don't do that. That's a bad idea. I can't..." Then she was on her feet and out the door before he could do anything to stop her.

He squeezed his eyes shut as pain tore through his chest. What on earth had possessed him to say something like that when he already knew she didn't want him? He was an idiot, just like the voices in his head had been telling him for years.

If he had been smart and bided his time with her, there was a small chance she would have accepted him in the end. But instead he had gone ahead and destroyed everything. She would avoid him from now on, and he wouldn't get a second chance to make this right. He had scared her away for good, and all that was left for him now was to try to pick up the pieces that were left of his heart.

Gawen let himself fall back on the bed. He was still naked, and the door was wide open, but he didn't care. Let the world see him in his pitiful state. Then the people around him could join the voices in his head to tell him how stupid he was. It was what he deserved after all.

He didn't know how long he had been lying there when someone entered the room. It was irrelevant who it was because he already knew it wasn't Nes. The footsteps down the hall had told him as much.

"Gawen." Henry's voice was low and held barely contained rage. "What did you do to my sister?"

Henry was his alpha, and it would have been polite to look at the man when he spoke, but based on what had just happened, the red-haired wolf wouldn't be his alpha for much longer. "I told her I'm falling in love with her."

Silence filled the room for several seconds before Henry spoke. "And are you?"

Opening his eyes, Gawen turned his head to look at Nes's brother still standing just inside the door. "Yes."

Henry let out a deep sigh, and his gaze dropped to the floor. "Shit. And she thinks you want to mate her. Yeah, that would do it."

Gawen sat up, concern making his muscles tense. "Do what?"

"Send her running." Henry lifted his head and met Gawen's gaze.

"What?" He was on his feet and moving toward the door in an instant, but Henry stepped into his path.

"She promised me to be back within the hour, Gawen. Amber is still hours away. Otherwise, I wouldn't have let her go." A muscle ticked in Henry's jaw. He clearly wasn't happy that Nes was out there on her own.

"Okay." Gawen gave a short nod and didn't make a move for the door, even though every cell in his body was telling him to go after his little bird. Her safety was paramount, but deep down he knew that seeing him would only send her running further away.

"Besides." With one eyebrow raised, Henry's gaze dropped to Gawen's groin. "You need to put that away before you go anywhere. Or you're going to have an issue with seven enraged mates, me included."

Gawen nodded before he turned to pick up his clothes from the floor. But instead of putting on his soggy clothes from before, he dumped them in a pile on the floor and went to get some new clothes out of his bag.

"Is she your mate?"

He froze at Henry's question. It wasn't one he had expected, and it wasn't a possibility he had seriously considered. He would have loved for it to be the case, but considering Nes was against mating, it was a good thing it wasn't. She had ripped his insides out by taking off, but as much as it hurt, he would have known if she was his. Wouldn't he?

"No." Gawen said the word with confidence, but it left a bad taste in his mouth, and the pain in his chest flared for a second. It was a good thing he was standing with his back to Henry with his face hidden from view, or his wince might have led the alpha to believe that Gawen wasn't sure about his answer.

Henry didn't say anything more, and Gawen finished dressing before he turned around.

Nes's brother studied Gawen's face for several seconds with an unreadable expression on his face before he opened his mouth. "For what it's worth, I think Nes is more taken by you than she wants to admit, perhaps even to herself. I'm not trying to be mean or tell you what to do, but I think you should have waited to tell her how you feel until you had spent more time together. She might still come around eventually, but knowing how you feel about here has scared her."

Gawen shook his head slowly. "I think I need to accept the reality that she doesn't want me. She might find me attractive, and perhaps she would have conceded to having a physical relationship with me for a while, but she doesn't want a mate, and she's never made that a secret." He sighed as pain stabbed through his chest again. "I just can't help how I feel about her. We barely know each other, but I already know that she's everything I've ever wanted."

Henry frowned. "Let me talk to her. Perhaps if I—"

Gawen shook his head again more firmly this time. "Don't. I don't want her to feel pressured. It will only make her more wary of me. If she changes her mind, she can come find me. But I doubt she ever will."

His alpha crossed his arms over his chest and looked like he wanted to argue, but he didn't say anything.

"And one more thing." Gawen fisted his hands at his sides at the sense of loss that threatened to send him to his knees. "When this is over, I won't be coming with you to be a part of your pack."

Henry's eyes widened. "May I ask why?"

Gawen swallowed to try to clear the lump in his throat. "You're her brother. Every day I see you I'm going to be reminded of what I lost, and I already know I won't be able to live with that reminder constantly."

His alpha narrowed his eyes at him. "Are you sure she's not your mate?"

CHAPTER 27

Nes

Nes would have loved to be able to change into her wolf and run, but that was impossible during the day. Particularly in an unfamiliar area like this. She had no idea where to go to avoid unsuspecting people, and she couldn't afford to be seen and cause a national wolf hunt. Not to mention the unwanted attention of the entire shifter community.

She lifted her gaze and stared out over the mirror-like surface of the sea loch. It was strange, considering the storm that had passed through the area not long ago. The calm almost felt unnatural and like a warning of what was to come.

Amber wanted to kill them all. And it was not an empty threat. The fact that she hadn't yet succeeded in killing anyone in their group was nothing short of a miracle. By all rights Henry should be dead and so should Sabrina, but they had both lived because of lucky circumstances that they had been unaware of at the time.

Nes was fortunate enough to still have her brother, and she hoped it would still be the case in twenty-four hours. But there was no guarantee with Amber coming for them all.

She squeezed her eyes shut and rested her head against the tree behind her. Thoughts of Gawen forced their way into her mind, even though she had been trying to think of everything else to keep them out.

He was falling in love with her, and the shock of hearing him say that had made her run away from him. But it wasn't for the reason her brother had assumed. It wasn't the thought of mating Gawen that terrified her. The reason she had taken off was how much she had wanted to throw herself into his arms and beg him to mate her immediately without caring about the consequences.

The gorgeous blond man already had her heart, and her heart and body were both screaming at her to mate him and make him hers forever. And that more than anything scared her shitless. If she stayed close to him, she might end up doing something reckless.

What if she woke up in the morning with a mate who realized he didn't really love her after all? That he had made a mistake. It would be too late to do anything about it, and she would be stuck with someone who would resent her for the rest of her life.

Mating wasn't like marriage. If it had been, she didn't think she would have been so terrified. Divorce wasn't a desirable outcome, but at least it was an option if things didn't work out as planned. There was no similar option available to mated couples. Unless you counted Amber as a viable solution, but that bitch would hopefully be dead by morning.

The worst part about this whole mess, though, was that she had hurt Gawen. His feelings were new and might not last long, but he thought he was in love with her, and there was no doubt that her rejection had upset him.

At least they weren't true mates, and he would soon come to understand that he was better off without her. He would find someone new, and perhaps in time so would she. A human man who didn't know anything about mating. Although that thought alone was enough to make her stomach roll.

Nes took a deep breath and stared out over the surface of the water again. She needed to put her thoughts of Gawen away and focus on what was going to happen when Amber found them.

Gawen was powerful, and the witch was unlikely to be able to resist the power she could gain from their mating. The fact that they had no intention of mating and weren't going to cooperate might have been an obstacle before, but with Amber stronger than she had been, who knew if they would be able to fight her if she decided to force them to mate. And if she couldn't force them, she was likely to kill them.

Pain lanced through her, and she staggered back against the tree. The image of Gawen's broken body lodged in her mind, and she gasped for breath. He couldn't die. Not him. She might have hurt him, but she couldn't watch him die. And she would fight with teeth and claws and everything she had to prevent that from happening.

She was suddenly in a hurry to get back. In order to

make sure Gawen stayed alive, she would have to be close to him and never let him out of her sight. At least not until the evil witch was dead and no longer a threat. Until then she would follow him like a shadow. And if that pissed him off, it was too bad.

It only took her ten minutes to get back to the house, and after a quick peek into the living room to check if he was there, she raced up the stairs to their bedroom. But Gawen wasn't in their room or the adjoining bathroom.

She stormed back downstairs before coming to a halt in the hallway. It was a big house with plenty of rooms where he could be hiding, and the logical thing to do would be to ask someone if they knew where he was. But she didn't feel like talking to anyone when she had just hurt one of their friends.

He could be anywhere and not just in the house. There was the garden as well as numerous other buildings on the estate. But would he venture out there after what happened with Amber?

The sound of something hitting the floor in the kitchen drew her attention. Someone was there, but considering how many other people were in this house, it wasn't likely to be Gawen.

She approached the room slowly and stopped just before the threshold to peek inside. The room was empty except for one person. Gawen.

He was standing with his side to her by the counter, staring down into a cup of steaming liquid. His shoulders were slumped, and his expression was nothing short of devastated.

She had to lock her knees to stop herself from going to him. Her muscles tensed with the need to throw her arms around his neck and tell him she loved him and that all she wanted was him for the rest of her life.

Gawen put the cup on the counter. His lips twisted, and he shoved his fingers through his hair in obvious frustration. "Stupid. I'm so fucking stupid. Why do I keep doing this to myself? No one really likes me. No one ever has. So why would that change now? I'm a hybrid freak of nature for fuck's sake."

He shook his head and swallowed hard. "But I'll never forget you, my little bird."

Her heart squeezed painfully in her chest, and she bit her lip not to make a sound. His last sentence was spoken like he knew she was there listening. But he obviously didn't, or she doubted he would have been talking to himself like that.

His words were heartbreaking, and she had a bad feeling he hadn't been exaggerating when he said that no one liked him. He was clearly different, and the shifter community didn't like different. Except her brother and his friends who were above petty judgment like that. And Gawen now had a home with her brother's pack. Or…

A disturbing thought crossed her mind, and before she realized what she was doing, she stepped into the room and moved toward Gawen.

His head snapped around to stare at her, a look of horror showing on his face for a second before he clamped his jaws shut and narrowed his eyes.

Taking a step to the side, he looked to the door behind her like he was planning his escape. But she followed his movements, placing herself between him and the door.

"I'm sorry, Gawen, but I couldn't help overhearing what you said." She kept her eyes on his and winced at the anger and hurt there. "You're still a part of my brother's pack, right?"

He stared at her for a few seconds before he shook his head slowly. "No, I'm not."

Her heart sped up. "Why? I know he wants you to be. He likes you." She took a step closer.

Gawen flinched, like she had just slapped him, and took a step back, bumping into the counter. "I..." His shoulders sagged, and he looked away. "He reminds me too much of you."

She froze as she realized what he was saying. He would leave the only people who accepted him because he couldn't bear to be reminded of her. Were his feelings for her really that strong?

He had looked devastated when she had run from him after his declaration of love, and again just a minute ago, but she still hadn't expected his feelings to be more than a temporary infatuation that would soon pass. But what if she had been wrong? Was she throwing away something unique by refusing him?

He took a step to the side before passing her on his way toward the door. But she couldn't let him go yet.

"Gawen." She clamped her hand around his wrist to stop him.

"Don't." He sighed before he looked at her. "I can't be around you right now. Just please stay in the house. Don't venture out on your own again. I'll be gone as soon as this is over. You won't have to see me again."

"But I—" She clamped her mouth shut and let go of his wrist. Telling him that she cared would only make this worse. Hopefully, his feelings were only an infatuation as she had first thought, and they would fade quickly.

But the thought did nothing to stop her heart from breaking as she watched him walk away.

CHAPTER 28

Aidan

Aidan scrubbed his hands down his face and let out a silent sigh. He hadn't meant to listen to the exchange between Gawen and Nes, but once Henry's sister showed up, he hadn't wanted to alert them to his presence.

He had walked into the large pantry, looking for a snack, just something to tide him over until dinner. Unlike some of his fellow enforcers, he could eat just about anything without any adverse effects.

When Gawen had walked into the kitchen, Aidan had been ready to walk out and talk to him until he had seen the raw pain in the man's eyes.

When he noticed Nes watching Gawen from the kitchen doorway, Aidan's chance to reveal himself was lost, and he ended up watching the brutal side of love play out right in front of him.

A single tear rolled down Nes's face when she

watched Gawen leave, and Aidan inwardly cursed. It was so obvious to him that those two belonged together, but it clearly wasn't as obvious to them. Or at least not to Nes. Something in her past was stopping her from grabbing onto the good thing staring her in the face.

Aidan wasn't surprised. He had watched it happen countless times before. And as much as he wanted to grab them both by the scruff of their necks and shake them until they saw reason, he couldn't. It wasn't his place to fix people's love lives.

And what did he know anyway? He had never been in their situation, and if he kept following the rules, he never would be either. An enforcer couldn't take a mate. It was one of the few things that could destroy them.

As soon as Nes left the kitchen, he exited the pantry. Duncan and Julianne had said they would make dinner, something quick and nutritious to make sure everyone was ready when Amber showed up. And Aidan planned to help them cook.

It wasn't his favorite pastime, and he paid people to do it for him at his London home, but then he was usually too busy to think about cooking and cleaning. His time was better spent making sure humans and supernaturals were safe from the truly nasty creatures out there, the ones too powerful and cunning to be easily handled by someone else.

Laughter preceded Duncan and Julianne's arrival in the kitchen, and Aidan let their amusement lift his own spirits. He hadn't been around Duncan for long before realizing that the big wolf was the clown of the party, and he particularly loved teasing his mate.

Leaning against the pantry door, Aidan crossed his arms over his chest and waited. He wondered how long it would take the couple to notice him if he stood perfectly still.

"Forget it, big boy." Julianne shook her head as she moved into the kitchen. Duncan followed right behind her with one hand on her ass. "The kitchen table is off limits, remember? Trevor was clear on that."

Duncan let out an exaggerated sigh. "But I've barely had a chance to kiss you since this morning. And everyone's too busy hashing out the details of the plan to check on us anyway. A few minutes is all I'm asking. I just need to feel you come on my cock. That's all."

Aidan rolled his eyes. Of all the people in this house, Duncan was the one who could most easily pass for a teenager. But his mate seemed to love his antics, even if she sometimes pretended not to.

Julianne's laughter filled the room. "You're insatiable. It's a good thing I can't get enough of your big cock."

A wide grin spread across Duncan's face. "Does that mean—"

"No." Julianne's answer was short and stern, but the width of her smile rivaled her mate's.

Aidan cleared his throat, and watched as their eyes rounded when they noticed him. "I'm here as your chaperon. I hope you don't mind. There was some concern that dinner might not be ready on time otherwise."

"Seriously? Who said that?" Duncan stared at him, clearly taken off guard.

"Me. Just now." Aidan chuckled. It was always fun

playing a joke on a joker.

Duncan's jaw dropped for a moment before he barked with laughter. "Fuck, you had me there for a second."

CHAPTER 29

Gawen

Gawen didn't have an appetite, but he knew he had to eat to keep his strength up. No matter what had happened between them, he was going to make sure Nes walked away from their fight with Amber uninjured.

Pushing his food around his plate, he tried to focus on the conversation around the table in the dining room, but it was no use. He could only concentrate for half a second at a time with the painful longing for his mate stabbing through him with every beat of his heart.

His whole body seized like he had just turned to stone. *Mate.* He had been so sure she wasn't, but he had been wrong. Nes was his. It was suddenly so clear. Why on earth hadn't he understood that before? He'd had feelings for women before, but they were nothing compared to his love for his little bird.

Forcing himself to breathe, he turned his head to look at her. She was sitting several seats down and across the table from him. Her spiky black hair was a bit messy, and there were dark shadows under her eyes. She looked tired and vulnerable, and all he wanted to do was take her in his arms and tell her that everything was going to be all right. That he would protect her and take care of her for the rest of her life.

But he couldn't do that. He couldn't even tell her she was meant to be his. It would only freak her out, and that was the last thing he wanted to do right before Amber showed up to kill them. Nes needed to focus on the task at hand, not worry about being his mate.

He pulled in a deep breath and sat up straighter. At least he had a purpose now. To protect his mate at all costs. Not that he hadn't already planned to protect Nes, but his determination to keep her alive had just increased tenfold.

Gawen wasn't going to hold out hope that she would one day accept him. But there was a small chance, and he was going to hold on to that like a lifeline through the fight. Because if one of them died, there wouldn't even be that small sliver of hope left.

Focusing on his plate again, he tried to remember the important aspects of their plan. He might be missing something since he hadn't been able to pay attention, but he thought he had an overview of the main parts.

They would be leaving for a small, secluded beach shortly, bringing a few things with them to be able to stay there comfortably until Amber showed up. Assuming, of course, that she showed up that evening or during the night, but there was no reason to believe otherwise.

Fia, Sabrina, and Steph had been working on some kind of blocking spell to try to prevent Amber from getting into people's heads. But since they hadn't been able to test it, they had no idea whether it would actually work. He suspected that the three witches had a few other things up their sleeves as well, though. Fia had already shown that she was good at protecting people against magical attacks, and perhaps the other two would be able to help with that.

Aidan hadn't given a lot of details of what he could do, but perhaps they would get a demonstration later. He was extremely powerful, perhaps even more so than Gawen had thought. It was easy to underestimate him since he seldom acted like he was more than an average supernatural. But then that was true for several people in their group.

Trevor and Bryson would be in their animal forms, wolf and panther respectively. They would be ready to attack Amber with teeth and claws and pull her into the water if possible.

Callum and Vamika would keep an eye on the area, using their surveillance gadgets, and warn them of Amber's approach as early as possible. The sooner they knew the witch's location, the sooner they could adjust their plans. So far the couple hadn't been able to pick up where Amber was on the road, so it was impossible to tell when to expect her arrival.

But judging from the bitch's fury when she forced her way into his head, Gawen didn't expect her to delay her attack. She wanted them all gone. And his taunting had only served to increase her determination to get rid of them immediately.

The two humans and the single vampire amongst them would be sticking together. It was early evening, and the sun was hovering low in the sky. But as soon as it dipped below the horizon, Eleanor would be able to throw off the blanket and help protect the humans. Henry and Duncan would both be there to protect them as well.

Leith and Michael would stay close to the witches to protect them and give them their power if necessary. If Amber ended up in the water, Leith and Sabrina would immediately follow and do whatever they could to drown her.

And he would be right there beside them. Drowning people was one of the things he was good at, after all. But until then he would stay close to Nes while using his magic to fight Amber in any way he could.

Gawen put his knife and fork down. He hadn't been able to eat much. But the few bites he had been able to force down would just have to be enough. It was time to go anyway.

They left everything on the table and headed out to the cars. It was about a ten-minute drive and then a few minutes' walk to reach the beach.

Gawen was surprised when Nes fell into step beside him as soon as he left the house. He had expected her to fight him when he told her she was to stay in the same car as him. But when he headed toward Trevor's car, she followed him almost like staying close to him was the natural thing to do.

His chest swelled with longing, and hope surged through him, making his breathing faster. But he quickly squashed those feelings. It wasn't the right time to let his stupidity take over and rule his actions. Whatever her reasons for choosing to stay close to him, they had nothing to do with her wanting to be his mate.

They rode in silence in the backseat of the car for two minutes before he turned to look at her. She was staring straight ahead, looking deceptively calm, but her white-knuckled fists in her lap gave her away.

"Relax and take a deep breath. You will be fine. I will make sure of it." His voice was so hard it sounded mocking in his own ears. But it wasn't the time to be soft. He had been soft and caring his whole life, and look where that had gotten him.

Nes unclenched her fists and took a deep breath before she turned to meet his gaze. "Your role isn't to focus on me. Amber needs to die, and you are powerful enough to make a difference. I can't fight her, but I'll do everything in my power to protect you while you fight."

Gawen was momentarily stunned, and his pulse suddenly beat in his throat. Was this her way of telling him she cared about him after all?

But like before, he quashed the hope that surged through him. This wasn't about him. It was simple logic and had nothing to do with her caring about him or not. Her focus was on winning this fight against Amber. Pure and simple.

But that didn't mean he was going to let her risk her life. "How do you plan to protect me against someone as vicious and cruel as Amber? She will have no qualms about killing you to get to me. What are you going to do about that?" He inwardly winced at the brutality of his words, but he needed to know. And if he scared her enough to make her take a back seat during the fight, that would make protecting her easier.

She didn't even flinch. "While she's busy killing me, you can kill her."

He felt all the blood drain from his face, and nausea rose in his throat. She planned to sacrifice herself for him, or more accurately for all of them. She had obviously concluded that he was worth betting on in this fight, and she would do whatever she could to improve his odds of winning.

Fuck. Gawen clamped his jaws so tightly his molars squeaked in protest. If only he could take her far away and lock her up to make sure she stayed out of harm's way. But unfortunately that wasn't possible.

Perhaps it was time to give her a little honesty. "If you intentionally put yourself in harm's way, my focus will be on saving you and not fighting Amber. I won't be able to help it."

She bit her bottom lip for a second before narrowing her eyes at him. "You'll just have to fight that impulse. Your job is to kill Amber, and that's what you have to do. I don't know what you are but remember Aidan's words. You are stronger than you think, and you might have more abilities beneath that gorgeous exterior than you're aware of. Now is the time to believe in yourself and fight with everything you've got and everything you didn't know you had."

For the second time in as many minutes, he was left speechless. Stronger. Gorgeous. Abilities. Was she trying to tell him something beyond the obvious? She clearly believed in him more than he did himself. If he killed Amber, would it be enough to convince her to give him a chance? Or did her faith in him have nothing to do with her feelings for him?

The urge to tell her they belonged together made his hands clammy. He wanted to scream and beg her to accept him, even though he knew it was a horrible idea and would be completely counterproductive. It would send her running so fast and so far he would never catch her.

The car stopped and Gawen looked around to see they had parked in a wooded area, but he could see the water in between the trees.

He didn't look at Nes as he got out of the car. She had obviously made up her mind about her role in the upcoming fight, and he had to come up with better arguments to convince her to change her mind.

"Follow me." Duncan's voice rose above the others, and Gawen turned to see the man waving to get their attention.

"You take this." Trevor handed him a large pack, and Gawen nodded as he accepted it.

They had packed some food and water and extra clothes before dinner. And Duncan had even gathered a couple of tents and a few sleeping bags for the humans among them. They all expected Amber to show up soon, but for all they knew she could have changed her mind about when to approach them. She had proven herself to be unpredictable at the best of times, so they were better off being prepared for anything when it came to her.

They moved in single file down the narrow path in between the trees. Gawen scanned the area around them constantly. No one spoke, but they still made enough noise that it would be easy for someone to sneak up on them without being heard.

The beach was about one hundred and fifty yards long and all white sand and clear blue water. Under any other circumstances, he would have loved to be there with friends. Genuine friends like these.

His life had completely changed in just a few days, but unfortunately, it was too good to last. He had faith that they would be able to defeat Amber, but that didn't mean it would happen without significant losses. In actual fact, it would be a true miracle if none of them died before this was over.

He turned to look at Nes standing not three yards away, busy scanning the surface of the water with a deep frown marring her beautiful features. She almost looked like she expected something or someone to rise from the depths and attack them. But the threat they were about to face wouldn't come from the water. In fact, the water was their friend. Or at least it was to some of them.

He wondered for probably the hundredth time if he should have told everyone what he was. It would have let them know they could rely on him in the water. But it might also give them a kind of false hope. They already knew about his magic, which could be used both on land and in the water, whereas his hybrid nature didn't give him much of an advantage out of the water.

CHAPTER 30

Nes

Nes kept staring at the inviting blue water, wishing this was a normal evening. The sea looked so inviting, and she would have given a lot to be able to wade in and swim into the sunset.

And if she were lucky, she might live to experience that another day. But if she wasn't... Well, there was no point thinking about that.

She turned to look at Gawen and stiffened when she found his considering gaze on her. He had been shocked and angry that she had decided to protect him against Amber at the cost of her life, if necessary. But as far as she was concerned, that was the best contribution she could make in the upcoming fight. She didn't have any special powers that she could use to make a difference against the horrible woman directly, but she might be able to provide enough distraction to allow Gawen to deliver a fatal blow.

His expression was unreadable when he slowly sauntered over to her. He was wearing a tank top and shorts, which did nothing to hide his perfect body, but he didn't act like he really understood how gorgeous he was.

Her body heated as her gaze traveled over his thick shoulders and arms, sculpted chest, and powerful thighs. *Damn, the man is a work of art.* It was still hard to believe that someone like him was falling for someone like her. How was that even possible?

He didn't stop until there was less than a foot between them, and she had to tip her head back to meet his gaze. "I want you to reconsider your plans to protect me, Nes. We will all be better off if you hang back and let me stand front and center and take the brunt of whatever she's got planned for us. If you approach her, I can guarantee you that your brother will rush in to save you and possibly get killed in the crossfire."

Fuck. Gawen had a point, and one she hadn't considered. But anger still boiled through her at him bringing it up. "Really? You're going to use my brother's life to force me to do what you want? That's low."

"But true, and you know it." His expression tightened and he stared at her defiantly. Leaning toward her slightly, he seemed even bigger than usual.

She should put him in his place. Come up with some snappy response. But for the life of her she couldn't think of anything to say. All she could do was stare at him.

The need to touch him was almost unbearable, and her need to kiss him even worse. She squirmed as her body grew hot. What was wrong with her? All hell could break loose at any moment, and all she could think of was how desperately she wanted to be close to this man. It was unnerving and shockingly stupid.

"Nes." Her name rolled off his tongue like a caress, and his eyes started glowing as she watched.

What would be the harm in kissing him? There was no guarantee they would both live to see dawn, and the least likely one to make it was her. And if that happened, would he be better off left with the knowledge that she loved him or the belief that she didn't? Which would serve him best when he was going to pick up the pieces and move on?

Before she could consciously decide what to do, she launched herself at him. Her legs wrapped around his waist, her arms around his neck, and her mouth crushed against his in a desperate kiss.

He staggered back a step before regaining his balance. Then, his arms crushed her to him, and he kissed her back like his life depended on it.

She poured all her feelings into the kiss. Her love for him, her determination that he would survive, and her hopes for a future that she would never really allow to happen even if they both lived. But he didn't have to know the last part. That knowledge would die with her.

Gawen suddenly tore his lips away from hers. His eyes were wide when he searched her face like he was looking for confirmation of what she had just tried to show him.

"I love you, Gawen." She let her emotions fill her eyes. "You're the most amazing man I've ever met."

Air whooshed from him like she had just punched

him in the stomach. And it took him a second before he pulled in another lungful. "I love you, little bird." Leaning his forehead against hers, he squeezed his eyes shut. "And I always will."

Until death do us part. Tears pricked the back of her eyes, and she clenched her teeth to hold them at bay. She knew what was likely to happen, and she suddenly questioned her rash decision to show him how she felt. Perhaps he would have been better off not knowing after all. Then there would be no reason to miss her and mourn what could have been.

He pulled his head back, and when she met his gaze, she was shocked to see hard determination. "And that's why you will stay in the background during this fight. I'll protect you, not the other way around. I won't allow you to risk your life for me, and I'll tie you up if I have to, to make sure it doesn't happen."

Her jaw dropped, and it took her a second to adjust to his sudden change from soft lover to hard protector. But she should have known he wouldn't change his mind about keeping her away from danger.

She gave him a sweet smile, but she knew her eyes were anything but sweet. "What exactly did I say to make you think you're the boss of me? I'll do whatever I think is necessary to keep you safe."

His eyes narrowed. "I will tie you up and—"

A chuckle sounded from behind her, and she recognized Duncan's voice. "I would tell you two to get a room, but it's not really the right time for that. Perhaps you should postpone this discussion until after the fight? I think we would all rather fuck than be here right now."

Gawen clamped his mouth shut, but his eyes were

still narrow with determination. She could see that there would be no point arguing with him. He wasn't any more likely to relent than she was.

"Approaching from the east. Four hundred yards." Callum's voice rang across the beach.

For a moment everything stopped, and silence reigned. Then movement and hushed voices sounded from around them as everyone hurried into position.

Her heart started pounding in her chest like a jackhammer, and the rushing of her pulse in her ears almost drowned out the sound around them.

Stark fear flitted across Gawen's face for a moment before his expression turned to stone.

Before she knew what was happening, he threw her toward the water, and she landed on her knees in the soft sand a foot from the water's edge.

"Stay behind me." Gawen's words and power slammed into her, almost knocking her back into the water. Instead of it being painful like she would have expected, heat blasted through her and robbed her of her breath. Her clit started throbbing with an almost painful intensity, and her pussy clenched as wetness soaked into her panties.

It took her a few seconds to get her lungs to start working again. And her whole body was so consumed by lust that her mind was struggling to make sense of what had just happened. She had experienced something similar before when he had come in her mouth, but then he had told her he was falling in love with her, and the implications of what had happened hadn't really registered.

To have someone's power affect you so profoundly was reserved for mated couples, and not even all of those experienced it. The fact that she was experiencing it with Gawen was a clear indication of what they were to each other.

She had thought her heart was hammering hard in her chest before, but it was nothing compared to what it was after realization hit. Her heart slammed against her ribs so hard she thought the poor things might splinter at any moment.

Gawen was hers. Not just a friend, or a boyfriend, or a lover, but her true mate. It explained why she had fallen for him so fast and why he had fallen for her.

A spell of dizziness made her plant her hands in front of her to stop herself from falling face first in the sand. The world was tilting on its axis as fear and disbelief almost choked her. This was too much. This couldn't be happening. She was supposed to be in control of her own life, not some fucking destiny.

CHAPTER 31

Nes

Destiny was happening, and even as Nes raged against fate's cruel hand snapping its fingers at her to obey, her protective instinct stiffened her spine and sharpened her mind. She felt an urge to destroy something to demonstrate against the unfairness of it all, but Gawen's safety took precedence.

He stood ten feet away with his back to her, scanning the shrubs and trees beyond the sand of the beach. The muscles in his shoulders and arms were bunched and ready, and his power practically vibrated in the air around him.

Amber would emerge onto the beach at any moment, and her mate was ready. But ready for what? It was impossible to predict what Amber would do once she appeared. She was there to kill them, but how she was hoping to achieve that with so many powerful people all focused on taking her down, Nes had no idea.

A man walked out from between the trees, and everyone seemed to freeze in their position.

The newcomer came to an abrupt stop when he saw them, his eyes widening in bewilderment and fear. And no wonder. Everyone was facing his way with body language clearly indicating that they were ready to attack.

This person wasn't the one they had been expecting, though, and after a few moments people started to relax.

The man swung his gaze from one to the other of them, clearly not sure what to do. His feet seemed rooted to the spot as he took in their mixed ensemble, emotions playing over his face ranging from fear and horror to confusion.

Aidan was the first one to approach the man. He sauntered toward the newcomer like they were just a regular group of friends out enjoying a normal summer evening at the beach.

The last thing they needed, and one of the reasons they had chosen this secluded beach in the first place, was innocent bystanders. And this man seemed to be exactly that.

As far as she had been told, Amber had never had an accomplice. Even Jack, who had intended to forcibly mate Steph, had never been anything other than a pawn in Amber's plans. But there was always the chance that this man was another pawn.

"Out for an evening stroll, are you?" Aidan's voice was warm, and there was a welcoming smile on his face. He reached out his hand in greeting when he was still six feet away.

"Yes." The newcomer's voice had a subtle tremor to it, but apart from that he seemed to be relaxed. He accepted the handshake as soon as Aidan was close enough.

"If you're looking for a place to be alone, it won't be here tonight." Aidan's voice was still pleasant, but there was a hint of annoyance in it that hadn't been there before.

The man tried to pull his hand back, but Aidan held on to it for a few more seconds before letting go.

If Nes had learned anything about the enforcer, it was that he didn't do anything without reason. She wouldn't be surprised if he had used that handshake to read the man like he had with the people in their group just a few hours ago.

"I'm... I can leave. I didn't mean to intrude." The man snatched his hand back as soon as Aidan let it go. Frowning, he stared down at his palm like whatever the enforcer had done had left a mark or at least a sensation.

"Oh no, I think you should stay. At least until we've had a chance to chat." Aidan's voice was no longer pleasant, and Nes could feel the power he was using to reinforce his words from where she was kneeling almost a hundred feet away.

Her unease trickled down her spine like cold water. What was going on? Why didn't Aidan want this man to leave? Had he felt something unusual when he touched the man, or was this just some kind of precautionary measure?

Gawen was still standing with his back to her and his face hidden from view. His body seemed relaxed, but she had no way of knowing what he was thinking.

She looked at the other people spread around the beach, but their expressions didn't answer her questions. Some of them didn't show any feelings at all, while others looked as confused as she felt. Whatever Aidan was doing wasn't universally understood among their group, but hopefully, they would get an explanation soon.

"Why don't you follow me?" The enforcer turned and headed toward the water, clearly expecting the man to follow without question.

The newcomer didn't move, and Nes expected him to suddenly make a run for it. But a few seconds later, he took a couple of tentative steps after Aidan before continuing at a quicker pace.

The enforcer had stopped just a few feet from the water's edge. His posture was relaxed as he stared out over the gently rippling surface. He didn't move a muscle until the other man came to a stop next to him.

"This is your unlucky day I'm afraid." Aidan crossed his arms over his chest as he turned to look at the man beside him.

The newcomer had already been pale, but at Aidan's declaration, his face went white as a sheet, and he took a step back, like he was preparing to run away after all.

"You won't get far, so don't even bother." The enforcer blew out a breath in exasperation. "We have no plans to end your life, but there is someone out there who will kill you without a second thought."

The man frowned and looked back at the place he had come from, like he expected someone to stand there waiting for him. Turning back to look at Aidan, he cocked his head. "I didn't see anyone on my way here. I'd rather just go home, if you don't mind."

Aidan shook his head slowly. "Unfortunately, I can't let you do that. You'll have to stay here until this is over. What's your name?"

The man stared at the enforcer for a couple of seconds before he answered. "Patrick. I'd rather just take my chances with whoever you think is out there. I can hold my own in a fight if I have to, and if it's only one of them…"

Aidan shook his head again. "She's not just anyone. Trust me."

"She?" A slight curl to the man's lips told of his amusement.

And there it was. Nes let out a barely audible huff. Patrick had seemed like a decent enough man until that moment. But one word was all it took to tell her exactly what kind of man he was. Someone who considered himself superior to women because he was physically stronger. He was the perfect example of the type of man she stayed well clear of. Or at least she had after having experienced firsthand how selfish and unpleasant a man like that was.

Moving her attention back to Gawen, Nes rose and tried to brush some of the wet sand off her knees. She had a million questions for him, but it wasn't really the best time to bring them up. Had he already figured out that they were true mates? And if so, why hadn't he told her?

Gawen suddenly spun around to face her, almost like he had felt her eyes on him. He closed the distance between them in a few long strides before taking her head in his hands and kissing her hard.

It was a short kiss, but one that left her lips tingling

and her breathing choppy. "Thank you for staying behind me and letting me protect you." The words were mumbled against her lips.

Nes put her hands on his forearms. The feel of his sinewy muscles under her palms was comforting. She wanted to tell him that her place was at his side and not behind him, but it would only ignite another argument between them. Instead, she nipped at his bottom lip, eliciting a groan from him.

"Little bird, if you're not careful, I might carry you into the water and have my wicked way with you."

His words and the gravel in his voice sent need rocking through her body, reminding her of what his power had done to her mere minutes ago. Her panties were already wet, and she had no doubt that the scent of her arousal was affecting him.

She chuckled. "Would you really want to fuck me in front of everyone?"

He pulled his head back until she could comfortably meet his shining blue eyes. "No, but I wasn't prepared earlier when you suddenly kissed me like you needed me more than oxygen. That kind of behavior can go to a man's head, you know."

"Which one?" She made a show of licking her bottom lip.

His gaze predictably dropped to her mouth, and he groaned again. "Both of them. What are you trying to do, distract me? Because it's working, and this isn't the time for that."

It was true, and she should stop, but everything inside her was yelling at her to claim this man. She had been adamantly against mating for so long, but when staring into Gawen's eyes, she was suddenly struggling to remember why.

CHAPTER 32

Gawen

Gawen's heart was beating wildly in his chest. Something had changed with Nes in the last couple of hours. She was looking at him like she couldn't get enough of him. And her earlier fear seemed to have vanished. Whatever had happened to instigate that change, he loved it, but he would still like to know what it was so he didn't accidentally trigger some kind of backlash.

"Gawen." Aidan's voice was clipped, like he was struggling not to snap. "Can you please come here a second?"

No, I can the fuck not. I'm busy. Can't you see that? But instead of telling the enforcer that, he let go of Nes with an apologetic smile and started toward Aidan.

Patrick's arms were crossed over his chest, and he looked mildly irritated. Which was a bit surprising, considering he had been almost ready to bolt in fear just minutes ago.

"I've tried my best to convey the risk of leaving here alone without going into too many details." Aidan rolled his eyes. "But this idiot would rather die than stay here apparently, and I'm about to let him."

Gawen nodded slowly while keeping his expression carefully blank. He could feel Patrick's shifter power. The man wasn't an alpha, but he wasn't weak either.

Gawen reached out his hand toward the man. "I'm Gawen."

Patrick's hand had barely touched his, when the shifter yanked his hand back with a look of distaste on his face. "Things like you don't belong around here. You should all get out of this area instead of giving me tales about some horrible woman who will kill me. What's wrong with you people?"

"What seems to be the problem?" Trevor's power prickled against their skin as he approached, and the change in Patrick's demeanor was instantaneous.

The newcomer's gaze dropped to the ground, and he seemed to be debating whether to kneel or not. "No problem, alpha. I didn't realize these were friends of yours. If I'd known, I—"

"You wouldn't have acted like an ass again?" Trevor shook his head like he was disappointed. "This isn't the first complaint I've had about your behavior, Patrick. Aidan here is trying to save your life, but quite frankly, I'm not sure you're worth it. Perhaps we should let you die. It might be better for everyone around here."

"What? But I..." Patrick's words died when he lifted his head, and his gaze landed on Jennie, who had just come to stand next to Trevor and taken his hand.

Recognition showed on Patrick's face before his eyes narrowed. "She's human."

Trevor nodded, his expression tightening. "She is. And she's also my mate. Any disrespect to her is a disrespect to me, and the same goes for all these people you see around here. They're my friends, Patrick."

Patrick pressed his lips together in a hard line and didn't say a word. But his expression was like an open book, clearly portraying his disgust.

Trevor stared at the man for a couple of seconds before he shook his head again and turned to Aidan. "Please tie him up. He's an asshole and few would miss him around here, but that doesn't mean he deserves to die."

Gawen didn't waste any time and grabbed Patrick and had him face down in the sand before the man realized what was going on. He sputtered and shouted profanities, but he wasn't strong enough to be a real challenge.

Aidan chuckled. "I'll get some chains."

As soon as they had the man secured at one end of the beach, Gawen returned to Nes.

She had spread a blanket out on the sand and was sitting there, watching the sunset, when he approached. His chest swelled with gratitude as he took in her beautiful profile. He hadn't yet had time to process the fact that he had found his true mate. It seemed too good to be true, and there was a nagging feeling between his shoulder blades telling him it was.

Her head turned, and a smile lit her face as their eyes met. "Are you going to join me, or are you just going to keep standing there?"

Shaking off the nasty feeling, he returned her smile. They might have one minute or ten or perhaps hours before Amber showed up, and he was going to enjoy every second of it.

He sat down behind her with one leg on either side of her, before pulling her back against his chest. Her hair tickled the side of his face. If sitting like this was all he ever got to do with her, he would be happy. Just being this close to the woman he loved was more than he had ever dared to hope for.

Leaning her head back against his shoulder, she reached up with one hand and buried her fingers in his hair. "I wish we were here all by ourselves. No people, no danger, just the two of us."

He smiled against her ear. "Me too, little bird. Me too."

She tipped her head back, staring up at him.

Cupping her chin gently, he leaned down and kissed her. It was a strange feeling with her head upside down with respect to his, but her mouth tasted just as sweet as it always did.

Sliding his tongue against hers, he lost himself in the sensations. His cock hardened fast, his body hot and restless. The mating bond was pushing him to claim his mate, but first he had to tell Nes that they were mates. And he didn't want to do that until Amber was dead and they could spend some quality time together.

She abruptly ended their kiss and got up. Then she moved over to one of the large backpacks and pulled out another blanket.

"Are you cold?" He watched as she walked slowly toward him while unfolding the blanket.

"No." She bit her bottom lip while amusement sparkled in her eyes.

Draping the blanket over his shoulders, she plopped her butt down between his legs while facing him before placing her legs beneath his bent knees. "Grab onto the corners of the blanket and put your hands on my shoulders."

He arched an eyebrow at her while he did as she requested. She seemed to have some kind of plan that required privacy, and he was curious and excited to find out what it was. Although, he wasn't sure whatever she had planned was a good idea out in the open.

"I have a few questions for you." She smiled at him.

"Okay." Gawen nodded as he studied her face for any indication of what they might be. Her smile was sweet enough, but he had a feeling she was about to make him squirm.

"But first"—she palmed his cock through his shorts—"I need leverage."

He groaned and tightened his grip on her shoulders. "What do you mean?"

Her hand was suddenly inside his shorts, her fist tightening around the base of his cock.

He closed his eyes as a shudder racked his body. She shouldn't touch him like this while they were sitting where anyone could walk up to them at any moment. The others might not be able to see what she was doing behind the blanket, but it wouldn't be difficult to understand what was going on anyway.

"I'm about to ask you a few questions, and I want you to answer me truthfully."

Gawen nodded. "I will, if I know the answers."

"Good." Her fist slid up his hard length before she brushed her thumb over his tip. "Did you know we're true mates?"

His eyes snapped open, and he stared at her with wide eyes for several seconds before he answered. "Yes." *But how do you know? And when did you find out?* He wanted to know, but he was going to let her finish questioning him first.

Her thumb circled the rim of his cockhead before pressing lightly against his frenulum, causing him to let out a low growl.

"How long have you known?" Her eyes narrowed a little, and her hand slid down to the base of his cock.

He cleared his throat. "Since dinner. I just suddenly knew."

Nes nodded slowly and brought her hand back up his rock-hard shaft until her palm slid over his tip and smeared the drops of precum that had leaked out around the head of his cock.

His balls tightened, and a shiver raced down his spine. He was already aching for release, and she had just started touching him. It was so slow, though, that he doubted he would come anytime soon. Was that her intention? What would happen if she asked him a question he couldn't answer?

"Were you going to tell me that we're mates?" Her eyes bored into his, and he realized his answer to this question was more important to her than the others.

"Yes." It was the truth. He had planned to tell her, just not yet.

Her hand slid up his shaft and over his head, catching more of his precum in her hand. Then, she tightened her fist and pumped her hand fast up and down.

Sweat broke out on his forehead, and his breathing hitched. All his muscles tensed as the impending pleasure sent warning tingles down his spine.

And then she stopped.

"Nes, please." He groaned and rocked his hips in desperation, but she removed her hand.

"When?"

Gawen stared at her serious expression for a couple of seconds before her question registered, but he had no idea what she meant. "What?"

She rolled her eyes. "When were you going to tell me?"

"I…" *Shit*. He had a feeling she wasn't going to like his answer. "After… After we kill Amber."

Her eyes narrowed again, and he jerked when she wrapped her hand around the head of his cock. "Why not before?"

He swallowed hard to try to control his voice. "Because you didn't want a mate, and I didn't want to freak you out right before the fight."

Her expression didn't change as she stared at him for what felt like minutes.

He was just going to ask her what she was thinking when she started sliding her hand up and down his hard length. Her pace was slow, but it was enough to make him shiver with how good it felt.

"Did you like my mouth on you?"

Her question took him by surprise, and the memory of her hot mouth on him was enough to send him over the edge.

Tucking his head against his chest, he snarled softly

as pleasure exploded through his system, and his cock jerked in Nes's hand. Trying to keep as quiet as possible, he rocked into his mate's hand until his orgasm faded, and his breathing started to settle.

"I take that as a yes. I love you, Gawen." Her whispered words in his ear made him smile, and he had to swallow to keep his happiness from clogging his throat.

He had thought she would get angry or take off again when she realized she was his, but she seemed to be fine with it. Perhaps even more than fine. "I love you, too, my little bird, and I plan to claim you as soon as we have taken care of Amber. Does that scare you?"

"A little."

He lifted his head and looked at her.

She shrugged and gave him a small smile. "But I know in my heart you're perfect for me and that we'll be good together. It's just hard to convince my anxiety of that."

CHAPTER 33

Nes

Nes's pulse was thundering in her ears. She hadn't been kidding about her anxiety. It was telling her to run, but in this case, it was wrong. She hadn't lied when she said Gawen was perfect for her. He was, but it might take her some time to relax into that knowledge.

"I'm a sticky mess." He grinned at her, his beautiful eyes back to their normal blue and no longer sparkling like jewels. "And you're a very bad girl for making me explode in public."

Chuckling, she inwardly thanked him for changing the topic. It was getting too heavy, and she needed to focus on something else to calm down. "Maybe. But it could've been worse."

Nes looked down at his softening dick in her hand. She had covered the head of his cock with his tank top just before he came, so the stickiness he was referring to was relatively contained. After wiping his cock and her hand with a clean section of his shirt, she tucked him back into his shorts.

His soft lips grazed her forehead. "Thank you. Looks like I have to lose the shirt."

"I think so." She smiled at him. "Sorry about that but it was better than the alternative."

Amusement filled his eyes, and he winked at her. "No need to apologize. I'm not about to complain about you jerking me off. But the next time, I would prefer you do it somewhere a little more private so I can return the favor. Your noises and expressions when you come are mine and mine alone. I can't do anything for you here where we're surrounded by people."

"You can kiss me." Putting her arms around his neck, she angled her face as an invitation.

"I can." His lips were warm when they molded to hers. The blanket hiding their bodies from view fell away when he cupped the back of her head.

Parting her lips, she let out a small sigh. The knowledge that this man was going to be hers for as long as she lived was both amazing and scary, but she was trying to focus on the amazing part. They might have just met, but he had already shown her he was different from the men she had known before. And the fact that her brother trusted him was another stamp of approval, even though she didn't need Henry's blessing to choose a man.

As if her thoughts had conjured him, her brother's laughter close by made her break the kiss and turn toward the sound.

Henry's grin was wide while his eyes darted

between her and Gawen. "Am I detecting a little more than acting between you two?" His gaze dropped to the wet patch on the front of Gawen's tank top barely visible from where Henry was standing, and he chuckled.

"Be nice." Eleanor smacked Henry's arm. "They don't need a patronizing brother and alpha bothering them."

"I know." Her brother's smile went from amused to sincere as his gaze settled on Nes. "But I can't help worrying about you, Sis."

"I'll take good care of my mate. I'd die before I let her down." Gawen's tone was hard, and his power sank into Nes and made her gasp.

Henry's gaze snapped to Gawen, and his eyebrows shot up so high they almost disappeared into his hair. "Mate?" Then his hazel eyes returned to her. "Really?"

A happy smile spread across Nes's face as she nodded.

"Yes. She's mine." Gawen's tone was like granite, and his shoulders were rigid against her arms.

"I'm yours." She buried her fingers in his hair and tried to turn his head back to her. When he didn't move, she leaned forward and kissed the corner of his mouth.

It was enough to snap him out of whatever emotion had taken hold of him, and he pulled in a deep breath before facing her. "I'm sorry, I didn't mean to get so…" He frowned like he couldn't find the word he was looking for.

"Possessive?" Tilting her head to the side, she studied his face.

He nodded. "Please don't let that scare you. I don't

think of you as property. But you're mine to protect and take care of, and everyone and everything feels like a potential threat at the moment."

Henry burst out laughing. "Welcome to the club. We've all been there so we know what you're going through. And it doesn't disappear after you've mated. Hell of a bad timing to find out you're mates, though."

"Tell me about it." Gawen sighed and shook his head as he stared into Nes's eyes. "I don't know whether to hope Amber doesn't show up at all, or that she shows up immediately so we can get this over with. Being stuck in this place with a lot of people right now is testing my patience."

"And I'm here to tell you your predicament is about to get worse." Henry gave them a tight smile. "You two shouldn't stay this far away from everyone else. We're all safer if we stick closer together."

Gawen lips pressed together in a hard line, and Nes had no trouble understanding his frustration. But as much as she hated to admit it, her brother was right.

"Fine." After grabbing her hand, Gawen rose and pulled her up with him. He yanked off his tank top and stuffed it into a side pocket in the backpack before stuffing the blankets in the main compartment. "Let's go."

It didn't take them long to reach the others gathered at one end of the beach. They had a fire going, and to anyone who didn't know them, they looked like they were relaxing and enjoying themselves. But the strain in their smiles and the tension in their shoulders told another story. This wasn't a pleasant get-together with friends.

Patrick was sitting with his back against a boulder

and chains wrapped around his torso and his wrists. The scowl on his face was nothing short of menacing, but he didn't voice his displeasure.

"Have you found out anything more about Amber's whereabouts?"

Gawen's question took Nes by surprise. She didn't know exactly what she had expected, but saying something about them being true mates would have been natural.

But knowing Gawen, that might be exactly why he had asked that question, to postpone any questions about their previous behavior and save her the stress of being put on the spot. And she couldn't help feeling a sense of relief at that.

The questions would come, she had no doubt about that, but if given the choice, she would rather tackle them after their fight with Amber.

"No." Callum shook his head. "She could be anywhere, but I wager she's closer than we'd like. It would be stupid to let our guard down."

A strange whining sound caught Nes's attention a millisecond before something hit the sand right in front of her. Gawen's hand was torn from her grip when she was flung backward.

She landed hard on her back, sand peppering her face and body. Covering her face with her hands, she held her breath as more sand rained down on her, and a strong wind ripped at her clothing and hair. It was like she was caught in a tornado, but she didn't think this wind was a natural phenomenon.

She twisted onto her side before rolling onto her stomach. After pulling her knees up beneath her, she started crawling while tucking her chin against her chest to protect her face from the sand biting into her skin. The wind roared in her ears, making her want to cover them with her hands.

But instead she kept crawling. It was like moving against a strong current, but she had to get out of the blast before she could do anything to stop whatever was going on.

Thoughts of Gawen and what had happened to him were rushing through her mind and telling her to go back to get him. But she forced the urge down. She wouldn't be able to help anyone with sand blasting her face. She couldn't open her eyes, and breathing was difficult, as she could feel the sand finding its way into her nose. The only chance she had was to get out of the storm.

It felt like she had fought against the wind forever, when her head suddenly broke through the outer wall of the tornado. She was about halfway down the beach, and the area looked exactly like it had before. The sand was completely undisturbed by the wind behind her.

Looking to her left and right revealed that there was no one else around. Nobody had made it out of the storm yet, or at least not in the same direction she had. But even if someone else had made it out, there were most likely people still stuck in the sandy hell, and she would have to find a way to get them out or stop whoever was causing this.

Nes got to her feet and headed toward the trees. There was only one person who would target them specifically and was powerful enough to pull something like this off. And although she had never heard of Amber being able to create windstorms, the woman seemed to constantly come up with new tricks.

It was possible that Amber was standing in the middle of the storm, but since the witch hadn't appeared before the tornado started, it was more likely that she was hiding in the trees and shrubs somewhere. And with the incessant roar of the storm, there was a chance Nes could sneak up on the evil woman without being detected.

"Not so fast, bitch."

The snarled words made her dive to the side and roll to get away. But she wasn't fast enough. He was on her immediately, and the rock hit her temple hard before she could turn her head away. Patrick's leering grin was the last thing she saw as she fell into blackness.

CHAPTER 34

Gawen

Gawen fought against the pressure on his mind. Amber was trying to force her way into his head and take over, but he knew without a doubt that if Amber managed to take over his mind, it would all be over. She would use him to tear everyone apart, and he wouldn't be able to do anything to stop her.

Pain like nothing he had ever felt before ripped through his mind, like a thousand knives were cutting into his brain. But using his magic, he forged layer upon layer of protection to keep her out. It felt like a never-ending fight, with her tearing layers away while he added them.

You can't fight me, and you don't want to. Her words reverberated through his head, like she had just shouted them directly into his ear. *You want to help me. You want to rule.*

But she didn't know him and that her words had

the opposite effect of what she wanted. He had never wanted to rule anyone or anything in his life. Having power over other people had never appealed to him, but having their affection, on the other hand, had. He would do practically anything to have people's real affection, friendship, and love. And throughout his entire life, he had thought of that as a weakness, but in this moment it was his strength.

Gawen let the knowledge that he mattered to his mate and new friends fill his mind and used it to fuel his magic. The wall around his mind strengthened, decreasing the volume of Amber's voice in his head.

A furious scream tore through his mind before the pressure fell away, and the pain faded. He had won the first battle, but it was unlikely to be the last.

When he became aware of his surroundings, he was lying on his back. Sand filled the inside of his mouth and his nose, and he felt like he was drowning in it. Flipping over onto his stomach, he covered his face with his hands before he tried to spit out as much as he could of the gritty substance. But even though we managed to get rid of some of it, it still coated the inside of his mouth and his throat, preventing him from breathing properly.

His mind and body were both screaming at him to find Nes, but unable to open his eyes without having them blasted with sand, he would be fumbling in blindness and wasting time.

Water. He needed water, and he knew exactly where it was. A part of him belonged in the life-giving liquid, and he could always feel where there was a body of water nearby.

He crawled as fast as he could toward the water's

edge, and he hadn't moved more than a few yards before he felt it cover his hands.

As soon as he was deep enough, he dived beneath the surface and swam with powerful strokes away from the beach while rinsing out his mouth and nose.

He broke the surface about a hundred yards from the shore and spun around. Like he had expected, the sandstorm didn't extend into the water. It was more local than he had assumed. The funnel of sand covered almost half the beach and from where he was bobbing in the water, it looked like it extended only a few yards into the shrubs and trees beyond.

But no matter how carefully he scanned the undisturbed beach and the surface of the water surrounding him, there was no sign of Nes or any of his friends. Either they had managed to get out and hide among the trees, or they were still stuck inside that unnatural storm.

This situation was beyond anything they had planned for. But he had to come up with a plan fast, or people would start dying. The possibility that someone might already have died tried to gain purchase in his mind, but he pushed it away. Thinking the worst wasn't productive, and he couldn't afford anything unproductive at the moment.

He studied the tornado as he tried to think of a way to battle the wind and the sand to get to the people stuck within it. But beyond finding a mask to protect his eyes and secure his breathing, his mind drew a blank. And locating someone who had a mask like that would take too long.

Which left him with one option. Find and kill Amber. He knew she was close by. He had felt it when she tried to take over his mind. And she was most likely hiding somewhere in between the trees where she had a clear view of the beach.

But how was he supposed to sneak up on a witch who had the ability to pinpoint his location? It felt a bit like trying to surprise someone in broad daylight in the middle of a football field. Not possible if the person was allowed to turn around. Unless there was a way to distract them.

CHAPTER 35

Aidan

Aidan inwardly swore. He hated surprises, particularly surprise abilities popping up left, right, and center. Was there anything this horrible bitch couldn't do? He had not believed her capable of whipping up a windstorm, but apparently, he should have.

As an earth elemental, he had the ability to draw power from the earth itself as well as plants and trees, and he could also manipulate the earth to a certain extent. It allowed him to expel the sand from his body, including his eyes, mouth, and nose, and keep it from getting any closer than a foot from his skin. But it wasn't enough for him to locate the people around him.

Drawing power from the earth beneath his feet, he tried to force the sand back down to the ground. Sweat coated his skin, and his muscles bulged as he worked, but no matter how hard he tried, he couldn't control the air and the myriad of sand and dust particles spinning around and preventing him from seeing the people around him.

He couldn't even imagine what Leith and Trevor and all their friends were going through battling the sand. But by choosing to save some of them, he might be sentencing others to death. It would take too long to get them out of the tornado, and even when he eventually did, Amber might move it to their new location.

The hopelessness of the situation made him regret that he had agreed with the other enforcers to go alone to take care of the rogue witch. Ronan, his fellow enforcer and air elemental, would have been able to calm the wind.

But none of them had expected Amber's level of evil and resourcefulness. And he still couldn't believe her increase in power in such a short time. He had never in his lifetime met anyone who had been able to evolve so quickly, and considering he was pushing two millennia, that was truly astounding.

He reached out with his power to try to locate Amber, but even though he could tell in which general direction she was, he couldn't pinpoint her exact location.

Forcing his way through the powerful wind, he headed in her direction. She was the cause of this, and the only way to stop this was to stop her.

He had just stepped out of the turbulent wind and into the calm air among the shrubs and trees, when the wind suddenly died, and he came to an abrupt halt. The silence was deafening until his hearing adjusted, and he picked up the sound of coughing and wheezing behind him.

After debating for only a moment, he abandoned his mission to go after the witch in favor of helping people recover.

The sight that met him made him wince. Sand was covering everyone, some of them barely visible below dunes of sand close to burying them alive. If he hadn't considered himself lucky before, he did now.

After hurrying over to the closest couple, Bryson and Fia, he used his magic to extract the sand from their eyes and airways. Then he moved to Duncan and Julianne.

Trevor was already on his feet, carrying Jennie toward the water, and Leith and Sabrina were stumbling after them.

"Where's Nes?" The near panic in Gawen's voice made Aidan glance at him before scanning the nearby area. Nes wasn't there.

CHAPTER 36

Gawen

Fear filled Gawen's stomach with icy fire. Nes was gone, and so was Patrick. And unfortunately, he didn't think that was a coincidence.

"How the fuck did Patrick get out of his chains?" The question wasn't directed at anyone in particular. It was more of an indicator of his despair than an accusation.

They couldn't have gotten far, though, and the only logical direction to go was up the hill toward the cars. The possibility that Nes was unconscious or seriously injured entered his mind, but he didn't let it linger for fear that it would send him into a complete state of panic.

Without waiting for anyone else, Gawen took off into the shrubs and trees, heading uphill. He had no way of telling where she was. They weren't even mated yet, and even mated couples didn't typically have the ability to sense where their mate was.

What the fuck did Patrick want with Nes? If he wanted to escape them, he would have been much faster on his own. Was he planning to use Nes as a bargaining chip to force them to give him something? Or was this all orchestrated by Amber? The thought almost made him stumble when his knees started to buckle beneath him, and he pushed it to the back of his mind to join all his other terrifying questions.

No matter the reason, Gawen was going to find the asshole and kill him for what he had done. No mercy and no regret.

The cars were still parked where they had left them, and there was no sign of anyone else there.

He came to a stop as his eyes scanned the area for any sign that Nes and Patrick had been there, but there was nothing. Squeezing his eyes shut, he fisted his hands at his sides as the reality of the situation registered.

He didn't know where Nes was, and he had no idea how to locate her. She couldn't be far considering the short amount of time that had gone by since he had last seen her. But if Patrick had put her in a car, she could be practically anywhere in Scotland in just a few hours.

"Fuck. I'm so fucking stupid." His rash decision to storm off without discussing his options with the others had robbed him of precious minutes to find her. As usual he had shown himself to be an idiot. *You don't deserve her. She would be better off without you. You're a pathetic excuse for a mate.*

"Gawen, what happened?" The terror in Henry's voice was like a kick to the stomach.

"Patrick must have taken her." The words almost sent him to his knees in despair. How could he have let this happen? He should have searched for her in that sandy hell instead of heading toward the water to save himself first.

"With Amber's help. Otherwise, he wouldn't have been able to break those chains and get out of the tornado. He wasn't that powerful on his own."

His alpha's words sent a new spike of fear through him. Just the thought of Nes being in the witch's clutches was enough to make his vision blur with sheer terror.

"No." Gawen's legs suddenly gave out beneath him, and he sank to his knees. "She's mine to protect. I need to get her back."

"And we will." The steel in Henry's voice was laced with power.

"Let me try to find her." Sabrina was suddenly directly in front of him and holding out her hands toward him. "Support me with your power and use your mating bond to help me locate her."

He took her hands as he stared up at her, already knowing that she was doing this more to comfort him than because she had a real hope of finding Nes. If his mate was anywhere near Amber, the witch would block their efforts to locate her. "I'll give you all the power I have, but we're not mated yet, so I'm not sure how much I can help you. And if Amber…" He couldn't even finish the sentence. It felt too much like confirming his mate's doom.

A small smile softened Sabrina's face, but determination hardened her eyes. "You're true mates. The bond is already there. Use it for all it's worth."

Gawen blinked up at her as he suddenly recalled Nes's words in the car. *Remember Aidan's words. You are stronger than you think, and you might have more abilities beneath that gorgeous exterior than you're aware of. Now is the time to believe in yourself and fight with everything you've got and everything you didn't know you had.*

He wasn't sure he believed all of that, but for Nes he had to. Because he might lose her if he didn't try.

"Okay." Nodding, he got to his feet. "But I want Aidan to help stabilize my power just in case."

"I agree." Leith's expression was tight with concern. Stepping closer to Sabrina, he put his hands on her shoulders. "And I will support you as well."

The blond witch turned her head to look at her mate over her shoulder. "Leith, that's—"

"Necessary for my sanity." Leith's green eyes had a faint glow in them, and his power prickled lightly against Gawen's skin. "I know you want to protect me, my angel, but I am strong enough to handle this. Let me."

Sabrina blew out a breath before nodding. "Fine." Her lips tightened like she wanted to say something more but stopped herself.

Aidan came forward and put his hands on Gawen's shoulders. Accompanied by their mates' grumbling protests, Fia and Steph stepped up on either side of Sabrina and put their hands on her arms.

"I'm ready." Sabrina closed her eyes.

Gawen immediately felt her pulling on his power, and he opened up to supply whatever she needed. Letting thoughts of Nes fill his mind, he tried to feel where she was, but it was like stumbling around in a fog. He had no idea where to go and no landmarks to guide him. She could be right next to him or miles away, and he would never be able to tell the difference.

"Stop doubting yourself and let your bond and power guide you." Aidan's voice was filled with power that sent a shockwave through Gawen's body.

He grunted. It almost felt like receiving an electrical shock. Pain rippled through his body as his muscles contracted. His heart clenched hard in his chest, sending a tidal wave of blood through his veins.

What the fuck? He was just turning his head to shout at Aidan, when something seemed to unlock inside him. Power like he had never known before poured from somewhere in his chest and filled his body all the way out to his fingertips and toes. Magic crackled inside him, bouncing against the inside of his skin like it was trying to get out.

Mate. He had thought he knew what it meant, but he suddenly realized that he hadn't. Not even close. Nes wasn't just a woman he loved and wanted to be his for eternity. She was a part of him, woven into every fiber of his being and etched into his soul. They were one, and he knew exactly where she was just as surely as he knew where he was himself.

Opening his eyes, he saw his glowing blue eyes reflected in Sabrina's. Everyone was staring at him, and he wasn't surprised. If they had felt even a fraction of the power he had felt inside him, they were probably wondering what the fuck was going on and why he hadn't tapped into that power before. But this was as new to him as it was to them.

He took a deep breath before turning to look at Henry. "I know where she is."

CHAPTER 37

Nes

The first thing Nes became aware of was the throbbing pain in her head. It was made worse by hanging over someone's shoulder as they walked. She wanted to shout at whoever it was to stop, but she didn't seem to have any control over her throat or mouth.

She tried to open her eyes, but they felt like they were glued shut. And trying to move her fingers didn't give any better results.

Fear rushed through her like ice-cold spiders running through her veins. She wanted to scream in terror, but it was like being stuck inside a soundproof black bag that allowed her to feel movement, but she couldn't see or hear anything, and no one could hear her.

"Put her down here." An unfamiliar woman's voice sounded from her right.

Hearing the voice pushed Nes's fear from the front of her mind to somewhere a bit further back. It was strange because there was nothing calming about the voice. It was hard and cold. But it showed her that she could hear just fine. It was her eyes and the rest of her that didn't work as normal.

"Are you going to heal her?"

The male voice sent shockwaves through her system as everything came back to her. Gawen, her mate. She had lost him in the tornado. But Patrick had somehow escaped, and he had hit her with a rock, knocking her out.

And here she was with Patrick and a woman she could only assume was Amber.

"Yes. Now put her down. Gently." The woman huffed in obvious frustration. "I wouldn't have had to do this if you had been more careful. You could've killed her, and what do you think I would've done to you then? Do you think I would've had any use for you if she was dead?"

Nes felt Patrick's body tense against her. "I... I'm sorry."

Amber sighed. "Whatever. It doesn't matter. I won't have to contend with you for much longer anyway."

"What do you mean?" There was a slight tremor in Patrick's voice, and Nes would have laughed at his fear if she could. *Not so cocky now are you, you stupid idiot.*

Whatever Amber had promised this man in return for kidnapping her didn't really matter. The witch was going to kill him soon anyway. Patrick hadn't realized that yet, but he would soon.

"That I'm getting fed up with you not listening.

Put. Her. Down!" The command was infused with so much power that Nes automatically tried to curl into a ball to protect herself. But of course, her body didn't respond.

Patrick's body jerked, but he finally reacted and put her gently down on the ground.

A surprisingly soft hand touched her temple and a tingling sensation spread through her skin and her scalp. The throbbing pain quickly subsided, and energy filled her body like she had just been given a potent energy drink.

Nes hadn't yet turned thirty and was still considered a young wolf, but she couldn't remember ever having felt this energized before. And it was a bit unnerving to know that it was all caused by Amber's magic. The evil bitch was on a mission to kill shifters, not rejuvenate them. And yet her magic was full of life-giving power. If only she had chosen to use it for good.

But Nes wasn't fool enough to believe Amber was doing this as an act of kindness. The only reason the witch was healing Nes was to be able to use her to gain more power.

A surge of relief filled her body. Gawen was alive. He had to be or there wouldn't be any point in healing Nes to prepare her for their mating. But where was he? Why hadn't they taken Gawen at the same time they took her? Surely, that would have been easier than trying to retrieve him later. Unless, of course, they had stashed him somewhere already. She didn't know how long she had been out. Perhaps it was longer than she had first thought.

The tingling stopped, and the hand disappeared

from her head.

"She should wake up soon. Keep her calm without causing any more injuries. Is that understood?" The anger in Amber's voice was enough to cause goosebumps on Nes's skin.

"Yes." Patrick's voice came from right next to her, as if he were kneeling beside her. "But it would be easier if I had some rope."

Amber's chuckle had nothing to do with amusement. "You don't, so use your imagination. If you have one." The sound of her footsteps faded as she moved away.

As far as Nes knew, she was alone with Patrick. But it was impossible to say for how long. She stayed still with her eyes closed while she debated her next move.

She could bide her time until Gawen arrived. He was stronger than her and perhaps together they could find a way to escape. But she had no way of knowing the shape he was in, and considering how strong he was, he was likely to be restrained somehow. And even if Nes got an opportunity to escape alone, she would never leave her mate behind.

It wasn't an option to give in to Amber's wish and mate Gawen. The witch would take their power and kill them in the process, like she had done to several other couples already.

Nes focused on keeping her breathing slow and even. The thought of Gawen in pain made her want to gouge Amber's eyes out, but attacking the witch would only make this worse. She needed to stay calm and come up with a sound plan.

There was a possibility the witch hadn't captured Gawen yet. But even if she had, Nes and Gawen would be better off without having to contend with both Patrick and Amber. If the wolf was incapacitated, Nes could hide nearby until Amber returned, and if Gawen didn't return with her, Nes would run.

She had no idea where she was, and until she opened her eyes, she had no way of finding out either. But as soon as she opened her eyes, Patrick would know she was awake and would take action to stop her. And he was stronger than her, even if he wasn't an alpha.

The whole situation was infuriating, but at least anger was her friend as opposed to fear. She could use that anger against Patrick. She knew he was right beside her, and she had the element of surprise going for her. But she would have to use it wisely. If she didn't incapacitate him immediately after revealing she was awake, he would overpower her, and she would lose her only chance at getting the upper hand.

Nes was moving as soon as she opened her eyes. One hand hit his throat, and the other dived between his legs before squeezing as hard as she could. Her grip wasn't as good as she had intended, but it seemed to have an effect.

His initial surprise was soon overtaken by a wheezing whine of pain. But instead of curling into himself to nurse his wounds like she had hoped, he grabbed her wrist hard enough that something crunched inside it, and sharp pain shot up her arm. His other hand was curled into a fist when it hit her temple, sending her back to the ground with stars bursting in her darkening vision.

She didn't lose consciousness, but it was a near thing. Curling up on her side, she cradled her damaged wrist and tried to get her foggy mind to work.

"Bitch." The word was little more than a hiss forced out through his bruised throat.

Opening her eyes, she blinked a few times before she could focus on him. He was lying curled up next to her, staring at her with a mixture of hatred and pain in his eyes. His hands were cupping his balls, an injury she hoped wouldn't heal too soon.

She needed to get up and run, but her head was still spinning from the blow he had landed.

"I'll make you pay for that as soon as I'm the king of the wolves."

It took her far too long to understand the implications of what he was saying.

No. Fear froze her body as she stared at him. She had been told how Amber had made Jack believe he would become the most powerful panther in the world once he mated Steph. It was obvious that Patrick had been served the same lie. And there was only one female who wasn't mated in their group. Her.

Nausea rose in her throat, the horror of what was going to happen causing a cold sweat to break out all over her body. *Gawen! Gawen, help me!*

But how was he going to rescue her when he didn't know where she was?

At least it probably meant they hadn't captured Gawen. Perhaps Amber had realized he was too strong for her to manipulate, or she was doing this out of pure spite. By forcing Nes to mate Patrick, Amber would effectively ruin both Gawen's and Nes's lives. And it would undoubtedly have an impact on Henry and his friends as well.

Her eyes landed on Patrick again. His face was still

tight with pain, but she doubted it would last long enough to prevent their mating.

There was one thing she could do, though. It might not work, but it was worth a try. Almost anything was at this stage.

"I hope you realize she's going to kill you. And me as well. You'll never end up king of anything other than gullibility."

His lips pulled up in a sneer. "She'll get power from our mating, but so will I. And you'll be my bitch. Although, I would've picked someone else to be my mate if I could."

It was clearly meant as an insult, but for some reason it made her smile. "Right back at you. I wouldn't have picked you if you were the last man alive."

The hatred in his eyes intensified, and he opened his mouth to say something, but she beat him to it.

"But none of that matters since we won't live that long. The only reason Amber is this powerful is that she has taken the power from several mating couples already before killing them. Haven't you watched the news lately? She didn't even bother to hide the bodies."

A flicker of uncertainty passed over his face. "She promised me."

Nes couldn't prevent the laughter that bubbled out of her mouth. "Yeah, and what do you think she told all the other couples? Think about it, Patrick. She's a power-hungry bitch. Why on earth would she allow someone else to gain power as well? You want to be king of the wolves. Would you let someone else become more powerful as well if you could stop it?"

The previous confidence and hatred in his eyes were gone, but so, unfortunately, was the pain. She was out of time.

"Just remember, Patrick, that you still have a chance at life and a mate who will do anything for you. But as soon as you mate me, you're dead."

Footsteps sounded from somewhere behind her, and Patrick's eyes widened a fraction when they landed on the person approaching.

"Got you where it hurts, did she?" The derision in Amber's voice had Nes biting her lip not to smile.

Hopefully, Amber's behavior would convince Patrick that she didn't have his best interests at heart. But it was impossible to tell with someone like him. He craved power almost as much as Amber did, and he might decide he would be better off trusting the witch than a wolf who hated him.

But Nes wasn't ready to give up just yet. She would keep working on his mind every chance she got.

CHAPTER 38

Gawen

Gawen was struggling to contain his instinct to go get his mate immediately. He knew where she was, but he also knew that Amber and Patrick were with her. If he decided to barge in and take her, Amber might decide to kill Nes before he could get to her. And that wasn't a risk he was willing to take.

The fact that Amber hadn't killed Nes already could only mean that she had a plan that depended on her being alive. And there were only two options he could think of. Either she wanted to make a trade of some sort, or she wanted them to mate in her presence to give her power. Both options would require some kind of meeting between them, or at least that was what he was counting on.

"I don't like this." Henry was pacing, his mate's gaze following his every move. "Why would Amber take Nes and not you if she wants you to mate?"

Gawen took a deep breath to try to stay calm before he answered. "She tried, but I managed to push her out of my head."

"You what?" Henry stopped and stared at him, and he wasn't the only one.

"Perhaps it had something to do with the distance between us, but I managed to say no and push her out."

"Which is more than anyone else has been able to do so far." Sabrina was studying him with her head tilted to one side. "Has she tried to get into your head since?"

He frowned. "No. What are you thinking?"

She narrowed her eyes while she studied his face. "I'm wondering whether you have blocked her completely."

"Meaning?" He cocked his head while he tried to figure out what she was thinking.

One corner of her mouth lifted in a small smile. "Meaning that she might not be able to tell where you are unlike the rest of us."

His eyes widened as he realized what she was saying. "I might be able to sneak up on her without her realizing." Then he frowned. "But I have no way to test that theory without approaching her, and I'm not willing to risk my mate's life like that."

Sabrina's lips stretched into a wide smile. "We can conduct a little test right here. You can hide somewhere in the area, and I can try to locate you. Make sure you do to me whatever you did to Amber to push her out of your mind. If I can still find you, it's safe to assume that she can as well. But if I can't…"

Gawen nodded slowly as hope made his heart

speed up. Perhaps he could save Nes without tipping Amber off as to what he was doing. "Okay, I'm ready."

Nodding once, Sabrina turned to look at the other people surrounding them. "To make sure I can't hear where Gawen hides, I want most of you to spread out and hide within about two hundred yards of here. Come back in ten minutes." She turned and buried her face against Leith's chest.

Gawen took that as his cue to start moving, and several of the others took off in different directions.

As he moved away, he tried to lock down his mind the way he had done to get rid of Amber's intrusive magic. After moving for a while through the trees, he veered off to the left and found a place to sit down behind a few boulders.

Leaning his head back against the rock, he closed his eyes and thought about his beautiful mate. She was still in the same place as she had been a few minutes ago, and he could feel that she was alive. But he couldn't really get a read on her feelings or well-being. Perhaps that was something that would develop after they had mated, like it had for the other true mates in the group. At least he hoped it would.

But first he needed to get Nes back and make sure she was all right. And she might need time to recover before she could even contemplate mating him. He had failed to keep her safe, after all, so it wouldn't be unreasonable for her to need time to forgive him.

You'll be lucky if she ever does. You don't deserve someone like her, and you know it. His body stiffened as the voices in his head started breaking down his confidence. He knew he shouldn't listen to them, but it was difficult not to when they only told him what he already knew. The truth he had been told his whole life.

"No. Not now." He opened his eyes and shook his head like he was communicating with another person and not his own insecurities. "Nes is my true mate for a reason. She wouldn't be if we weren't perfect for each other."

Gawen conjured all the positive memories he had of Nes and let them flood his mind. Her moans when he kissed her. Her body writhing in his arms as the orgasm he had given her tore through her body. The love shining in her eyes when she told him she loved him.

He was going to work every day to be the best mate she could ever have. But first he needed to save her.

He rose when he was sure ten minutes had passed and started to make his way back. Sabrina hadn't come to get him, and hopefully, that meant she couldn't find him.

As soon as he stepped out of the trees, the blond witch smiled at him. "You're good. I couldn't even get a sense of the area you were in. You could have been in Japan or Peru, and I wouldn't have known it."

He grinned. Finally, it seemed something was going his way, and he was going to make the most of it.

CHAPTER 39

Nes

Nes watched as Amber paced. The witch seemed irritated, but she hadn't told them why.

Patrick was sitting next to Nes on the ground, having been specifically tasked to keep an eye on her. But Nes had made no move to escape since Patrick almost knocked her out again.

Hopefully, she would get a chance to speak to Patrick alone one more time. He had been quiet since Amber came back, but whether that was because he was afraid of the witch, or he was thinking about what Nes had told him, was impossible to say. Perhaps it was neither, and he was just waiting.

Amber suddenly stopped before she turned and headed straight toward her. Nes had to clamp her jaws together not to scramble backward. "What happened to your boyfriend? What did he do to increase his power? And don't tell me nothing. I know something happened to him."

Nes stared up into Amber's green eyes darkened by rage. The witch was looming over her, and her magic was oozing out like an invisible toxic cloud.

Her mind was searching for a plausible answer, but there was none. She wasn't even aware that Gawen's power had increased, but the witch seemed certain it had. "I only met him yesterday. As far as I know his power hasn't changed since then. But I'm no expert when it comes to magic."

Amber's lips curled in disgust. "You only met yesterday, and you've already decided to mate." She gave a dark chuckle. "Or decided isn't correct is it, since you're true mates. You don't have a choice. Or at least you didn't."

Nes started when the witch let out a sudden bark of laughter. Why was she surprised that Amber knew they were true mates and was still planning to force her to mate someone else? It was exactly what the witch would do to punish Gawen and demonstrate her power to everyone else.

"They're true mates?" Patrick's voice was filled with shock.

Nes didn't turn to look at him but kept her eyes on the lethal woman in front of her.

"Does it matter?" Amber's gaze narrowed as it moved to Patrick. "You will be the strongest wolf alive before dawn. Who your mate is won't matter. You can get all the pussy you want when you're that powerful. Isn't that what you want?"

"I... Um... Yes."

Nes inwardly cheered at the lack of conviction in his voice. Perhaps he was finally realizing what an idiot he had been to believe Amber in the first place.

"But what will happen to the true mate bond when we mate? Will our bond just replace it, or will she die when she can't be with her true mate?"

Patrick's questions made Nes turn to stare at him. Those were awfully good questions that she hadn't even considered herself. And she didn't know the answers, because she'd never heard of a situation like that, probably because the true mate bond, once identified, was always respected.

"Your bond will replace the true mate bond." Amber's mouth twisted with disgust. "Why all the questions all of a sudden? You were happy enough with this arrangement before. But I'm sure I can find someone else who would like to be king of the wolves if you're having second thoughts." A confident grin spread across Amber's face.

"No, I'll do it." Patrick's response was immediate, but his eyes were wide and his body tense. He didn't look confident in the least.

"Good." Amber spun and walked a few steps away from them before turning back and crossing her arms over her chest. "Then I think you should get ready."

All the blood seemed to leave Nes's head, leaving her lightheaded and nauseous. *Not yet. Not yet.* She had wanted another chance to persuade Patrick not to go through with it, but she was suddenly out of time. It was really happening. In just a few minutes, she would lose Gawen forever.

At least she was lucky that she wasn't going to live long enough to mourn that fact. And hopefully, the bond would be severed like Amber said, leaving Gawen free to live on and find someone else who would love him like he deserved.

"Ready, as in undressing?" There was a tremor in Patrick's voice, and it had nothing to do with excitement.

"Yes." Amber threw her hands in the air in exasperation. "Do I have to explain to you what mating entails? Or will you be able to complete the act without step-by-step instructions? Fuck, you're stupid."

Instead of answering, Patrick got to his feet and started undressing.

Amber shot Nes a pointed glare.

Bile rose in Nes's throat as she got to her feet. She took her time loosening the knot of her shorts before slowly pushing them down her thighs. Her loose T-shirt reached her upper thighs, covering her sex.

She should have mated Gawen right there on the beach, ignoring everyone around them. Someone might have told them to stop, but they would have backed away and left them alone as soon as she told them Gawen was her true mate.

If only she had realized who he was earlier, but the truth was she would have backed away in fear instead of embracing the gift she was given. She had spent years fueling her fear of mating, and it was still itching at the back of her mind, even though she knew Gawen was a dream come true.

She shuddered as the horror of what was about to unfold sank into her mind like a lead ball. Dreams were only temporary, and she had no choice but to face the reality of this situation. Nothing and no one could save her now. It was too late.

"On your hands and knees." Patrick's voice was

clipped and emotionless.

She didn't look at him before facing away from him and sinking to her knees. Her panties were still on because she hadn't been able to make herself remove them. But she had no illusions about a scrap of material being enough to stop him.

Her stomach roiled as she sensed him sinking to his knees behind her. All she had to do was stay still and let him do what he wanted. The possible physical pain didn't scare her. It was the consequences that had her feeling numb with fear and devastation. She might throw up as he raped her, but it wouldn't stop him or Amber from following through with their plan.

Amber took a step closer, and Patrick's fingers dug into her right hip.

"No!"

The word and the voice reverberated through her just as Amber was flung backward into a tree. A loud crack sounded as the tree shook and the trunk split, sending half of it to the ground.

Gawen rushed toward her with his eyes shining like blue lightning and the muscles in his upper body rippling with power. He looked bigger than he had before, but that might be due to her position on the ground before him.

Relief flooded her body, and she grinned as she rose to her feet. But apparently her perceived victory was too soon.

Something hit Gawen in the middle of his chest, blackening his skin and making him stagger. His face twisted with pain before his eyes dimmed and his expression relaxed into an emotionless mask.

Nes stared in horror as Amber rose and moved

toward Gawen with a slow nonchalance like she had all the time in the world. A menacing smile spread across her face before she turned her piercing gaze on Nes.

"Don't stop on his account. He will enjoy the show." The evil cackle that left the witch's mouth sent chills down Nes's back.

A hand landed on her shoulder and tried to push her back down. But she was unable to move, her body frozen as she stared at Gawen's blank expression. It was bad enough to be forced to mate someone other than her true mate, but to have him watch it happen was infinitely worse.

"Get on with it!" Amber's power hit her like a blast from a furnace, and Nes automatically took a step back, crashing into Patrick's body.

She shuddered at the unwanted contact and tried to take a step forward. But Patrick used the opportunity to push her to her knees.

"I will torture him until you comply." Amber bared her teeth in a nasty grin before waving her hand in Gawen's direction.

Nes watched in horror as the skin covering his upper abs started to bubble and split before the burns crept slowly down his belly toward the waistband of his shorts. There was no mystery what would happen if she didn't let Patrick mate her.

Tears filled her eyes and blurred her vision as she went down on all fours, but she quickly blinked the tears away and kept her eyes on her gorgeous mate. Whatever happened to her, she was going to keep her eyes on him, to show him that he was the only one who mattered.

Patrick's hands clamped onto her hips a moment before his groin connected with hers.

She sucked in a breath of surprise, making Amber chuckle. But the witch wouldn't have been so happy if she had known the reason for Nes's reaction.

Patrick kept bumping his pelvis against hers, even grunting like he was actually enjoying himself, but her panties were still in place and the man was as limp as a noodle.

CHAPTER 40

Gawen

Stop! Stop! Gawen's whole body was on fire, and it had nothing to do with the wounds covering his chest and belly.

His beautiful mate was being violated right in front of his eyes, and he was locked in his mind, unable to do anything to prevent it.

Her eyes were locked on his, but instead of pain, accusation, and hatred, they were warm with a love so profound it would have sent him to his knees if he'd had any control of his body.

He had thought his newfound power enabled him to block Amber from his mind, and it did to a certain degree. Except she had seized his body instead, preventing him from moving. Even his eyes were under her control.

And now another man was about to claim Gawen's mate as his own, and all he could do was watch, his heart breaking for what Nes was going through.

You don't deserve her. You're not even strong enough to protect her. She's better off without you.

And it was all true. He wasn't good enough. But he had never thought his failure would have such horrible consequences for someone else. Whatever happened to him didn't matter, but Nes was everything.

"I love you." The words were spoken softly but hit him with a force like a freight train at full speed, making him flinch.

Nes's eyes widened for a second before her whole body tensed, and she screamed at the top of her lungs. "I love you, Gawen."

He had been told once that words have power, and although this situation might not be what the person had been talking about, Gawen would never doubt that wisdom again.

Whether it was the actual spoken words that did it or Nes's wolf power accompanying them, he didn't know, but something shifted inside him, and power exploded through him and out of him.

Amber stumbled back before closing her eyes and turning her head away like she had been blinded.

Patrick crumpled into a heap behind Nes.

And his true mate's mouth fell open, her eyes filling with awe as she took him in from head to hooves.

Gawen knew what his mate was seeing. He had seen his own reflection in the water, and knew he looked like a large horse. And except for his sparkling blue eyes, he could be mistaken for one.

But he was something entirely different and vastly more dangerous than a normal stallion. And the power that had unlocked inside him was on a whole different level than it had been before.

Amber's eyes were filled with malice when she turned back to look at him. "I like the surprise, but you are still nothing compared to me. You are still a hunk of meat that can be cooked like everyone else."

Her magic shot out like a ball of fire. It was visible to him in this form, and with his increased speed, he effortlessly batted it away with a small blast of his own magic.

The witch followed it up with a series of powerful shots aimed at various parts of his body, but he batted them away as easily as he had the first one.

Her face contorted with rage before she suddenly changed tactics and turned toward Nes instead.

Continuing to deflect the magic fireballs from their target, he quickly moved until his body was shielding Nes from Amber's view.

But Amber wasn't deterred and kept up her assault by curving her magic around his body, aiming for his mate.

It quickly became a status quo with her shooting magic and him deflecting it.

He needed this to end before Nes got hurt. But he couldn't attack Amber while he was busy neutralizing her attack on Nes.

Sudden movement to his right drew his attention for a millisecond, but that was a millisecond too long. A ball of magic sailed past his head and Nes let out a scream of pain behind him.

His vision blurred as instinct took over, and he screamed his rage. Wrapping his magic around Amber like a cloak, he pulled water from half a mile away and filled her lungs until she choked.

The witch's green eyes grew wide with pain and disbelief as she squirmed against the tight hold he had on her. Her power was pushing against his, and he was struggling to keep her from breaking away when familiar magic filled the area around him.

Gawen could feel Aidan just a few yards away as the earth moved around him. Roots shot from the ground and wrapped around Amber's body, and boulders tore from the earth and rolled on top of her to pin her in place. Then the earth folded in on itself and swallowed her into its depths.

The shock of what had just happened held him captive for a second before he lifted his gaze in question to Aidan.

The enforcer gave a short nod, and it was all the confirmation Gawen needed before he shifted back to his human form and stormed over to his mate.

The sight that met him made him stumble and fall to his knees at her side. The left side of her chest and belly was torn open and the exposed flesh was charred to a crisp. Her head had rolled to the side, and her eyes were dull and lifeless.

Gently, like she could still feel pain, he lifted her into his arms and pressed her to his chest. They might have saved the world from an evil witch, but he had lost the most precious being in the world in the process.

Grief tore open his heart, and he welcomed the agony. It was nothing more than he deserved. He had failed to protect his mate, and for that he should suffer until life eventually left him. It wouldn't take long, not nearly as long as he deserved.

"I love you, Nes. Please forgive me." He whispered

the words into her black hair as he prepared to get to his feet.

Something snapped in his chest, an audible crack. His back bowed and his head was thrown back as light suddenly burst from his chest and swirled around him and Nes in a spiral toward the sky. The light was warm, like a perfect summer day, and a feeling of profound love suffused his being.

Nes's body convulsed in his arms, and the shock almost had him drop her. Light was still pulsing from his chest when he looked down at his mate's face. But the light wasn't just pouring out of him to swirl around them, it was pouring into Nes, making her skin glow like the light was filling her body to the brim.

He could only stare as the charred pieces of her heart turned into supple muscle and knitted together before her splintered ribs covered the organ. A steady thumping started as flawless skin sealed her wounds and erased the evidence of what Amber had done to her.

When he raised his gaze to her face again, her cheeks were rosy like she had just been taking a nap in the fresh air, and not died from a fatal wound that he should have prevented.

The light slowly faded, making him realize that they were still in the dark forest. Unable to take his eyes from Nes's face, he tried to make sense of what had just happened. He had healed her, which was an ability he had used many times. But that wasn't all. He had somehow restored her life as well. Only, it shouldn't be possible. He had never heard of anyone who could bring someone back from the dead. As far as he knew, his father didn't have that ability, and neither did any of his ancestors.

"Is she..." There was careful hope in Henry's voice when he sank down to his knees in front of him.

Gawen nodded, not sure if he could speak without his voice cracking. His whole body was so full of all kinds of emotions that he didn't know whether to laugh, cry, or scream. It was difficult to process everything that had happened in the last minute, let alone the last hour or day. His body felt numb, and words were inadequate. But he knew one thing. He wouldn't let go of Nes until she begged him to.

CHAPTER 41

Gawen

Gawen's eyes were trying to close, and he had to constantly peel them back open. Judging from the light outside, it was already past midday, and he hadn't slept a wink since bringing Nes back to Trevor's estate. And he wouldn't either until he could verify she was completely healed and not suffering from any lingering pain or discomfort.

He let his eyes travel down her body as she was lying tucked against his side in bed. He had dressed her in one of his T-shirts, leaving her panties and bra in place.

She had yet to wake up, but her breathing was calm and steady, and her heart rate was even. He had let his magic search her body for any unhealed injuries several times already, but she was healthy. There was nothing wrong with her that he could find. But he still couldn't stop worrying.

Tightening his arm around her, he pulled her closer. It wasn't really her health that was worrying him anymore, at least not her physical health. His main concern was how she would react to him when she woke up.

He was the one who had let her get killed, and he couldn't expect her to forgive him for something like that. It didn't really matter that he had somehow brought her back to life, when he was the one who had failed to keep her safe in the first place.

His heart clenched painfully in his chest. It was a miracle that his true mate was alive, and he should be beyond happy about that. But it was overshadowed by the fact that she might hate him when she woke up. And that would have been painful enough if they were a regular couple, but as true mates they wouldn't be able to postpone their mating for long without serious consequences.

It was an issue he didn't have a solution for. How could he let her mate him if she didn't want to? But on the other hand, how could he let her go when he knew she would suffer? He would agree to just about anything to earn her forgiveness. But it might not be enough after what he had put her through.

∞∞∞∞∞

Nes

Nes came awake, smiling. An arm was draped across her waist, and a large warm body was pressed against her side. And she knew exactly who it was who was holding her. Her true mate.

She opened her eyes and turned her head to look at

him. But her smile immediately faded from her lips when her gaze landed on his face.

Gawen's breathing was even. But there were deep lines marring his gorgeous face that shouldn't be there in sleep. He didn't look relaxed. He looked extremely tired and worried.

She frowned as she tried to recall what had happened before she fell asleep, and her eyes widened when memories started to filter into her still-foggy mind.

Amber. Patrick. Gawen. *Holy hell.*

If what her mind was telling her was true, Gawen could turn into a horse. And not just any horse. A large, beautiful creature with blazing blue eyes, a shiny brown coat, long black mane, and hooves the size of dinner plates.

Scrunching her face up, she tried to remember what had happened after he had changed. But no matter how hard she tried, her mind was blank. It was almost like she had blacked out in the middle of it, but she couldn't remember any reason why she should have.

There was no doubt, however, that Gawen had saved her from Amber and Patrick. And considering it was daytime, that was hours ago.

Staring at Gawen's face, she debated whether to wake him or not. He looked so tired, but he didn't look like he was getting the rest he needed.

After coming to a decision, she put her hand on his cheek and spoke softly. "Gawen."

His brows pushed together in a frown, but he didn't open his eyes or show any signs he was awake.

Burying her fingers in his hair, she tried again a little louder. "Gawen."

His eyes blinked open before focusing in on her. Then he pushed up on one elbow and studied her face like he was looking for something. But he didn't say anything.

Her heart sped up as he continued his intense scrutiny. What was wrong with him? He looked like something bad had happened, and he was trying to find out what she remembered.

Her fingers fisted in his hair. "Henry. Did something happen to my brother?" She stared into his eyes, searching for any evidence that she was right.

His eyes widened, and he jerked like her words had snapped him out of whatever he had been contemplating while studying her. "No. Henry's fine. Everyone's fine."

She sighed in relief and pulled her hand from his hair to put it on his arm that was still wrapped around her waist. "Then what's wrong? Did Amber escape again? It's not like that hasn't happened before. If everyone's fine, we will just have to try again."

A small smile finally curved his lips. "Amber is gone. Destroyed. Swallowed by the earth. She won't ever bother anyone again."

Returning his smile, she cocked her head. "Swallowed by the earth? It almost sounds like you mean that literally."

His smile widened. "I do. Aidan used his remarkable abilities, and that's exactly what it looked like. The earth claimed her. And Aidan assured me she's dead, and her body has already been broken up into a million pieces."

Nes stared at him and waited for him to tell her he was joking. But when his smile faltered, she realized he was telling her the truth, however unbelievable it sounded.

"She's dead. The witch is finally dead." Laughter bubbled out of her mouth. "Then why on earth did you let me sleep for so long? We should be celebrating."

Sadness crept into Gawen's gaze as he lifted it to stare out of the window. "You needed the sleep to fully recover."

"Recover?" She lifted an eyebrow at him in question, even though he wasn't looking at her. Was that why she couldn't remember anything that happened after Gawen turned into a horse? It made sense.

"You…" His voice choked off, and he cleared his throat before trying again. "You died. I got distracted, and Amber killed you."

Nes frowned at his words, but the haunted look in his eyes told her he was speaking the truth. Or at least what he believed to be the truth. "But how is that possible? I'm clearly alive."

She paused for a second. "I am alive, right? Or is there something else I should know? With everything I've seen and learned in the last few days, I don't really know what is impossible anymore."

His gaze came back to hers. "You're alive. And if it's any consolation, I don't know what's impossible anymore either."

She chuckled, the craziness of their conversation suddenly hitting her. "I think you better tell me everything that happened from when you changed into a horse."

"Not a horse." He shook his head slowly. "A

kelpie. I'm a wolf kelpie hybrid. My mother was a wolf, and my father is a kelpie."

CHAPTER 42

Nes

"So you're a mythical creature?" Nes cocked her head. It made sense that he was something out of the ordinary. "I know what a kelpie is according to Scottish folklore, but I'm not sure if what I've learned about them is accurate. You have to tell me more about that side of yourself, but first I want to know what happened last night."

He nodded and let out a deep sigh. "Amber attacked me with magic, but I was able to deflect her shots. So, she started attacking you instead. I managed to protect you until I saw movement in my peripheral vision and got distracted. One of her balls of potent magic hit you, and I heard your scream, but I couldn't go to you, or she would have used the opportunity to hit you again. By the time Aidan killed Amber and I could check on you, you were already dead." The tendons in his neck were taut, and his eyes were filled with anguish.

Gawen was clearly agonizing over what had happened to her, and it was likely one of the reasons he hadn't looked peaceful in his sleep. For some reason he felt responsible for her death, even though she was sure he had done everything in his power to prevent it.

He needed her to reassure him of his innocence in what he believed was her death, but she needed to know the end of the story before she could do that.

"I'm alive, though. So how did that happen?" She smoothed her hand along his forearm, enjoying the feel of his sinewy muscles against her palm.

"I…" His eyes dipped to her chest. But there was no heat in them, only confusion. "I'm not entirely sure. Light suddenly burst from my chest and poured into your body. Your shredded heart healed and started beating again. I have no explanation for what happened or why. And I have no idea whether I could do it again, or if it was something that happened just because you're my true mate."

Her jaw was slack when she stared at him with eyes so wide she probably resembled one of those green aliens from the old magazines. She should probably say something. Thank him perhaps. But what did you say to someone who had brought you back from death? She had experienced a lot of things in the last few days that she had never known were possible. But this was beyond any of that. This was the stuff of gods.

"Please say something." He stared at her with so much sadness in his eyes that it brought tears to hers. "I know I fucked up, and I know I don't deserve your forgiveness. But I'm begging you for it anyway. I can't live without you, Nes. You're the beginning and the end and everything in between. Without you everything is dark and cold."

She had to swallow before she could find her voice. "I thought you looked like an angel in the car yesterday. The only thing you were missing were wings. But then I changed my mind later on and decided you looked like a god. And now you just confirmed my suspicion. You *are* a god."

"No." He sighed and averted his eyes. "A god wouldn't have let you get hurt and die in the first place. A god would've made sure you weren't captured. A god would've kept you safe and not let you get raped." A shudder passed through his body, and his arm tightened around her waist. "I failed you on all counts. Even if I somehow managed to give you your life back, I was still the reason it was taken. One positive thing doesn't cancel all the bad ones."

Raped. Her eyes widened. Gawen still thought Patrick raped her. She hadn't even considered that possibility since it never happened.

Smiling warmly, she reached up and put her hand on his cheek. "Patrick didn't rape me."

Gawen's eyes snapped back to hers, his brows pushed together in a frown like he didn't believe her. "But he—"

"He pretended. Probably because Amber would've killed him if she realized that he couldn't."

He cocked his head. "What do you mean he couldn't?"

Her smile widened. "His dick was soft. I think I must've scared him when I told him Amber would kill us both as soon as we were mated. And I still had my panties on. Didn't you notice?"

Gawen nodded. "I noticed, but I thought he had just…" He winced.

"Pushed them out of the way?" Nes chuckled. "He could have, but he didn't. His dick never touched me."

"Thank God." Gawen leaned forward until his forehead was resting against her chest.

She buried her hands in his hair and just enjoyed having him so close, something she'd never thought she would be lucky enough to experience again. Her own true mate. What were the odds? And she loved it, loved him.

Something wet soaked into the front of her shirt, and Gawen let out a shaky breath.

"Gawen, are you…all right?" She had been about to ask if he was crying, but shifter men didn't cry and would be deeply offended if someone ever asked if they did.

"I'm sorry." The words were mumbled against her chest before he lifted his head and turned away from her. But not before she saw the wetness in his lashes.

She steeled herself before asking the question she probably shouldn't, but she had to know. "Why are you crying?"

His body tensed for a second before he sighed. "I'm sorry to disappoint you. I know you deserve better."

His words when she had watched him in the kitchen the day before suddenly came back to her. *I'm so fucking stupid. Why do I keep doing this to myself? No one really likes me. No one ever has.*

Tears rose in her eyes for him. Her mate was

broken, much more broken than she was herself. And yet he was so strong and compassionate. In time she would ask him about his past but not until his heart had healed from what had happened the night before. What he needed now was her unconditional love and acceptance.

She smoothed her hand up his arm beneath the sleeve of his T-shirt. "I love you, Gawen. I love all of you."

His throat was working, but he kept his face turned away from her.

Smiling, she drew a heart with her fingertip on his bicep. "Your smile and your laughter shine more light into my life than the sun ever has. I didn't want a mate, because to me mating represented control and dominance. But I want you. I want you more than I've ever wanted anything. I want all of you, including your smile, your laughter, and your tears."

He finally turned to face her, but instead of the smile she had hoped to see, his expression was carefully blank. "Why? I haven't done anything to deserve you."

She pulled her hand out of his sleeve before tapping her index finger against his breastbone. "You have done everything to deserve me. Treated me with love and respect since we met, and done everything in your power to protect me."

He flinched and opened his mouth, but she continued before he could object.

"But there's one more thing I need you to do for me."

He nodded without any hesitation and before asking what it was.

Licking her bottom lip, she flattened her hand against his chest. "Claim me."

His eyes grew wide, and he tensed. "Are you sure you want that after what happened last night? We can wait. Even if he didn't...remove your panties, he violated you. I don't want you to force yourself to be intimate again before you've recovered. We can talk to someone who knows about these things, and—"

"Stop." She shook her head at him. "I'm fine. But I need your lips and hands on me to erase every trace of last night from my memory. And I want to feel you come inside me and see the pleasure on your face when you do. Please make me yours. We're meant to be, and our life together starts right now."

CHAPTER 43

Gawen

Gawen's chest swelled as he searched her face for any evidence of fear or reluctance, but all he could see was determination and sincerity.

It was difficult to believe everything she had just told him, but he couldn't dismiss it as lies either. She had been against mating when she first met him, but the reasons for that had nothing to do with him. And she had warmed to him quickly, even though she had originally wanted to keep him at a distance. And that was before realizing they were true mates.

Pushing his insecurities to the back of his mind, he smiled at her. "You want me to claim you? Why don't you claim me instead? Use me for your own pleasure and make me your mate. Do whatever you want to me."

Gawen rolled onto his back and stretched out on the bed beside her. By giving her control, she could do whatever she felt comfortable with after her horrible experience the night before. His own mating bond was pushing him to take control and get this done, and he might give in at some stage, but not until he was convinced that she was as fine with this as she said she was.

Nes got up on her knees beside him with a teasing smile. "If that's what you want."

His heart sped up when she grabbed the hem of her T-shirt and pulled it over her head. Then she rose to her feet and quickly shucked her bra and panties before placing one foot on either side of his chest, giving him a spectacular view of her pink pussy.

Need slammed into him, turning him rock hard in an instant. "Are you going to undress me, or do you want me to do it?" He had planned to show some patience and let her call the shots, but his body was suddenly an inferno of desire, threatening to burn him alive.

His respect for those who managed to control their need to mate for several days grew. He would have done it for Nes without complaint, but it would have been adjacent to torture.

Nes grinned down at him. "I would, but I'll leave you to do it while you chase me to the shower." Before her words had fully registered, she was off the bed and halfway to the bathroom.

"Fuck." In one move he was on his feet at the foot of the bed with his T-shirt ripped from his body. Pushing his shorts down his thighs, he ran for the bathroom. But he hadn't taken more than two steps before he realized his mistake. His legs caught in the fabric, and he pitched forward with his nose aimed directly for the hardwood floor.

Catching himself on his hands before his face hit the floor, he kicked the shorts from his legs. Then, he jumped up and ran into the bathroom.

He stopped as soon as he crossed the threshold, taking in the naked glory that was his mate. There were seven other men in this house who considered themselves the luckiest men alive having found their mates, but he had them all beat. His mate was the most stunning of them all.

Standing with her back to him, she turned on the shower and held one hand in the spray while waiting for the water to heat.

"Have I told you how beautiful you are?" He crossed his arms loosely over his chest and leaned one shoulder against the wall.

Turning her head to look at him, she chuckled. "I'm not even close to being the most gorgeous person in this room. That's one of the reasons why I keep comparing you to angels and gods."

Shaking his head slowly, he walked up behind her and smoothed a hand down her spine. "I love your short, spiky hair. It showcases your high cheekbones and slender neck. And your body has just the right balance of curves to muscles for me, making you look strong while not sacrificing your feminine form. But I'll love you just as much, if not more, when your physical appearance changes with age, because your true beauty resides in your head and your heart."

After turning toward him, she put a hand on his chest. There was a tremor in her voice when she spoke. "I've never felt seen and valued by any man before you. No one has ever tried to find out who I really am. I know it's only been a few days, but I feel like you already know me better than anyone ever has." She put a hand on his cheek, staring into his eyes. "I hope I can do the same for you, that I'll be what you need in a mate."

Reveling in the love in her eyes, he leaned forward and kissed her forehead before smiling down at her. "You're already everything I need, little bird." He grabbed the bottle of shower gel and dumped a generous amount in his hand. "Will you allow me to clean your body? I can't pretend I'm not getting impatient to make you mine."

"Oh, so that's what this means." She shot him a wicked grin before wrapping a hand around his hard cock. "You can clean me all you want as long as I get to play with this." After giving his shaft a squeeze, she took the bottle from his hand and poured shower gel all over his dick.

"Sure." He choked out the word when she curled her fingers around his hard length. Sweat broke out all over his body when she started moving her hand up and down, her thumb rubbing against the sensitive area right beneath the head with each pass.

Gawen couldn't move. He could hardly even breath as he watched Nes's face and body language as she pleasured him. Her breathing was elevated, and her lips were parted as she stared at his cock with hunger heating her blue eyes.

He wasn't going to last long, the tingle of impending pleasure already licking up the base of his spine. The need to push into Nes's tight pussy and make her his was overwhelming, but he kept himself still to let her do whatever she wanted.

Her other hand reached between his legs and cupped his balls. They were already aching with the pressure of near release, and her soft hand massaging them pushed him closer to his climax.

"The pictures of you jerking off has been playing on repeat in my head almost constantly since I walked in on you." She licked her bottom lip before lifting her gaze to his. "But I love touching you more than watching."

He groaned. The knowledge that she had enjoyed what she had seen sent his need spiraling, and pleasure suddenly tore through him, taking him by surprise.

He roared her name as his cum painted her breasts and throat, the sight feeding his deep-seated need to mark her as his. Clamping a hand on her shoulder, he locked his knees as his orgasm rode him hard.

CHAPTER 44

Nes

Nes held her breath as Gawen's thick cock jumped in her hand and covered her skin with his seed. She loved the way his eyes lost focus as the orgasm claimed him, and her name roared for everyone to hear made her push her chest out with pride.

This man was hers, and they were about to make that official and permanent. She couldn't wait, her anticipation causing all her nerves to tingle with eagerness.

Gawen's body finally relaxed, and he pulled in a ragged breath before a sexy grin curved his lips. "I'm sorry I never got around to cleaning your body. But I can do it now if you want." Licking his lips, he lifted an eyebrow in question.

She shivered at the promise of pleasure in his eyes. "Yes please."

He dumped more of the shower gel in his hand

before leaning in and giving her a quick kiss on her lips. Pulling back, he stared into her eyes. "If at any point you want me to stop just say so, okay?"

"I don't think I'll ever want you to stop, Gawen." She smiled up at him, basking in the love and compassion in his eyes. She had a feeling he would spoil her rotten if given half a chance. But then, she felt the same about him. She wanted to make sure he had everything he could possibly want.

"Good." His lips brushed against hers in another quick kiss before he took a step back. "Now let's see where to begin." His gaze slid slowly down her body, lingering a little on her breasts and the apex of her thighs before continuing downward.

Nes shivered as heat gathered in her lower belly. She was already wet from touching him and watching him come. If he had wanted to enter her right away, she would have been ready.

Her gaze dropped to his still-hard shaft seeming to consider her with its one-eyed stare. Or perhaps not. He was longer and thicker than any man she had been with before, so perhaps a little preparation was wise.

"If you keep staring at my dick like that, this cleaning session might end up shorter than I had planned." His teasing voice brought her eyes back up to his, just as he smoothed his lathered-up hands over her shoulders and down her arms.

Butterflies seemed to take flight in her stomach. The fact that she could easily drive her mate crazy with need was a heady feeling.

He was so much bigger and stronger than her, and yet she had so much power over him. It was both wonderful and a little strange. Was this how mates typically felt about each other when the mating was based on love? Or was it exclusive to true mates?

"I can see I need to up my game here. Your mind seems to be wandering."

She blinked her eyes to refocus on his face. "Just thinking about the dynamic of mated couples. It's so different to what I thought, and we're not even mated yet."

"What do you mean?" Concern made his eyebrows crease, and his hands stopped moving.

Realizing she was frowning, she let a happy smile spread across her face. "Nothing bad. Just that love is a power all on its own, binding people together and making their difference in physical strength inconsequential. I've never considered that before. I always thought men were dominant in relationships because of their larger size."

Gawen's face smoothed into a loving smile. "I can tell you right now that I'll never be able to say no to you irrespective of what you ask of me." He pursed his lips. "Or that's not completely true. I'll say no to anything that puts you at risk, but apart from that, you have me firmly wrapped around your little finger."

She believed him. Both because of how he acted with her and because of how all the other men in the house acted with their mates.

Large hands cupped her breasts, and whatever she had been thinking was purged from her head with the influx of glorious sensations.

Letting out a drawn-out moan, she leaned into his warm hands.

He let out a low chuckle as he massaged her breasts. "That got your attention. I'll make sure to remember that."

His lips covered hers, and she tipped her head back to give him better access to her mouth. She gasped when he pinched her sensitive nipples, and he used the opportunity to fill her mouth with his exploring tongue.

She kissed him back, rubbing her tongue against his and enjoying his taste and texture. Kissing had always been one of her favorite parts of a relationship, but in her experience it wasn't something men cared for outside the early seduction phase. But for some reason, she didn't think that was true with Gawen.

He rolled her nipples between his fingers, sending sparks of pleasure directly to her clit, like there was some kind of direct connection.

His hands suddenly disappeared from her breasts, and she whimpered into his mouth in protest. But instead of taking pity on her, he broke their kiss with a chuckle and proceeded to rub his hands up and down her back. "As much as I'd like to keep cleaning your breasts, I have to wash the rest of you so I can eventually get you back to bed."

She laughed, but it ended on a strangled gasp when his hands suddenly dove between her legs. One hand slid between her ass cheeks and the other skated over her clit.

He grinned as he studied her face, no doubt finding her cross-eyed look entertaining. "Ready for a thorough scrub down here?" His fingers played over her sensitive nub, teasing her with just enough friction to make her pussy clench but not enough to satisfy her need to come anytime soon.

"Please. I need more." The words were out of her

mouth before she could stop them, and she immediately froze. If there was anything she had learned, it was that men didn't like to hear anything that might be construed as criticism of their skills in the bedroom.

But Gawen just laughed before leaning in and nipping at her earlobe, sending sparks of pleasure between her legs. "I know you do, and I'll deliver. But a little teasing never hurt anybody. In fact I think I like making you a little desperate for me to give you what you need."

Without warning, he grabbed the detachable showerhead and aimed the spray directly at her aching clit.

She cried out in shock at the intense stimulation and tried to take a step back, but Gawen's arm was suddenly wrapped around her hips preventing her from moving away.

"Gawen," she gasped and tried to wriggle out of his grip, but his arm was like a thick steel band holding her exactly where he wanted her. Until he wasn't.

He suddenly let go of her, and she stumbled back a couple of steps until she hit the wall.

But her relief was short-lived. As soon as he had reattached the showerhead, Gawen dropped to his knees in front of her. His mouth latched onto her tingling clit and sucked like she was an icicle on a scorching hot day.

She yelped and automatically tried to close her legs, but he had her locked in place as he went to town on her swollen nub.

Two fingers breached her entrance and pushed inside her, and her knees almost buckled when he started pumping them into her while lapping at her clit.

Gawen clearly had enough experience to know exactly what to do to push her toward her climax, and a small sting of jealousy pinched her heart. But she quickly pushed it away. If anything she should be thanking those women for the invaluable lessons he had learned. Nes knew what arrogance and inexperience in bed felt like, and she would never have to suffer through that again.

"Look at what I'm doing to you," Gawen growled against her pussy, and the vibration made her shudder.

She met his glowing blue gaze and sucked in a breath at the sight of him staring up at her from between her legs. It was naughty and hot, and made her feel sexy and confident.

Keeping her gaze locked on his, she widened her legs to give him better access.

His mouth was busy, but his eyes gave away his smile, and it felt almost as good as verbal praise.

Heat suddenly erupted from low in her belly, pleasure filling her body.

Gawen's fingers rubbed the extra sensitive area inside her and exquisite ecstasy pulsed through her system.

She would have landed on the floor if she wasn't held up by the wall and Gawen's tight grip on her.

CHAPTER 45

Nes

When Nes finally came down, she opened her eyes and found Gawen grinning up at her.

"I love that look on you."

She cocked her head in confusion. "What do you mean?"

He chuckled as he rose to his feet. "That flushed and satisfied look suits you, and if I have my way, I will get to see that every day."

Laughing, she put her hand on his sculpted chest. "I have a favorite expression as well."

"And that is?" He raised an eyebrow at her.

"The slightly cross-eyed look you get when you come."

Laughter burst from him. "I think you might get to see that often in the future. I'm not going to be able to keep my hands off you for any length of time." His eyes narrowed. "And while we're on the subject…"

Leaving the sentence hanging, he maneuvered her under the spray of the shower. "Rinse off and get into bed. I'll be there in thirty seconds."

After he poured shower gel into his palm, his hands flew over his body, covering himself in lather while she quickly rinsed her body of the remaining soap.

He had just made her come hard with his mouth, but her body was already heating with the expectation of what they were about to do. It would be their first time together and their mating baked into one. It was both nerve-racking and exciting, and both feelings were making her heart slam against her ribs.

After quickly drying off, she hurried to the bed and ducked under the covers. She suddenly wanted to hide, the whole situation making her feel awkward. What if she wasn't good enough? What if he was disappointed and didn't want to be her mate after all? Or perhaps he wanted someone else to satisfy his needs after they were mated?

"Now where is my beautiful mate-to-be?" There was amusement in his tone, but the roughness of his voice spoke of his need. "I think she might be hiding from me."

The covers were suddenly flung back, making her squeal with equal parts anxiety and excitement.

Her emotions must have been clearly visible on her face, because instead of lying down, he sat down next to her and put a hand on her arm. His gentle smile turned his face into that of an angel. "If you're not ready, we can wait. I won't do anything you don't feel comfortable with. Your feelings are more important to me than anything else. So, if you don't feel ready, that's completely okay."

Nes couldn't take her eyes off him. He was by far the most gorgeous man she had ever met. And it was enhanced by his loving and compassionate nature. He had never once disrespected her or done something that was exclusively for himself.

She suddenly couldn't remember why she was doubting him. Why she was doubting herself and their bond. True mates meant that they were perfect for each other. No other person in the world would suit her better. Or him.

Letting her face reflect everything she felt for him, she shook her head. "No, I don't want to wait. I want to claim you, so we can start our life together as mates. I deserve you and you deserve me. And we're going to spend many years of happiness together."

His grin widened as she spoke, and as soon as the last word passed her lips, he bent down and kissed her.

It started as a gentle movement of his lips against hers, but it soon turned into a frantic dance of tongues. She didn't even notice that he had moved until his weight settled on top of her.

His knee pressed between her legs, forcing them apart and opening her up to him. Their kissing had made her wet and ready, and she couldn't wait to have him fill her.

He lifted his head and stared down at her, his blue eyes glowing like a fire was lit behind them. "Are you ready, little bird? I'll be as gentle with you as I can, but my mating instinct is riding me hard right now, so you'll have to tell me if you want me to slow down or stop."

Nes nodded before smoothing her hands down his back to his ass. "Just fuck me, Gawen. I don't want gentle. I want to feel you fill me until all I can think of is you and what you're doing to me."

"I think I can manage that." His hips settled between her thighs, his cock hard against her clit. He ground against her, coating himself in her juices.

Digging her fingers into his ass cheeks, she widened her legs. "Please. I need you."

He chuckled, before he lifted off her and sat on his heels between her legs. His hand wrapped around his erection and gave it a couple of tugs as his eyes zoomed in on her wet center.

She couldn't help the moan that left her. "What are you doing? Aren't we—"

"We are." Winking at her, he shoved the other hand beneath her ass and lifted her until he could place the head of his cock at her entrance. "I want to watch as I stretch you to accommodate me. You're so tight. I can't wait to have you clamp down on me as you come."

Nes swallowed hard as she stared up at him. A smidgen of anxiety caused an icy trickle down her spine. She couldn't help wanting to be the best he'd ever had, but how could she when she couldn't come from penetration alone?

"Rub your clit, little bird. Let me see you play with yourself."

He smirked when her eyes widened in disbelief. Had she heard him correctly? Did he really want her to touch herself in front of him? No one had ever wanted her to do that before. Was that even normal?

"Do it." His gaze moved from her eyes to her pussy. "It's one of the sexiest things I know, to watch a woman pleasure herself. Have you ever done that for a man before?"

"No." She shook her head, still trying to accept that he was serious about what he wanted her to do.

"Good. Then I'll be your first and only. If you're planning to do what I told you." Tilting his head to the side, he gave her an amused grin.

She nodded before giving him a slow smile. If he wanted a show, she was going to give him a show.

Keeping her gaze on his face, she put her hands on her breasts. His eyes immediately zoomed in on what she was doing, the glow in them intensifying as she tweaked her nipples before smoothing one hand down over her belly.

He growled when she slid a finger over her swollen nub and then down over the head of his cock perched at her entrance.

His hips bucked forward like he'd momentarily lost control, sinking his hard shaft a couple of inches inside her.

She gasped at the sting of the intrusion.

CHAPTER 46

Gawen

"Fuck." Gawen's gaze shot to Nes's face, taking in the wince of pain. "I'm sorry, I didn't mean to do that. Do you want me to pull out?" He hoped she didn't. She needed to adjust to his size if this was going to work, but he had meant to take it slow. He just hadn't been prepared for how sexy she looked when she was teasing him.

Shaking her head, she gave him a tight smile. "No. Just stay still for a moment. I've never been with someone quite like you before."

He wasn't surprised. Most men weren't as big as him, not even shifters. But he wasn't worried that it would be a problem. They wouldn't have been true mates if they didn't fit. But as she had just pointed out, she needed time to adjust.

"Play with yourself. It will help." He gave her what he hoped was an encouraging smile while he kept his body in check. Need was pounding through him unlike anything he had felt before, and his instinct to make her his was threatening to take over.

She slid the pad of her finger over her clit, slowly, tentatively, like she wasn't sure exactly what to do. But her pace soon increased, and she started rocking her hips against him.

He took that as his cue to start moving. After pulling out, he pushed slowly inside her while gauging her reaction.

Her deep moan made him smile, and he pulled out almost all the way before sinking into her a bit farther than before.

"More." Her finger was working herself faster.

He complied, his next stroke settling him about halfway inside her tight pussy. His breath shuddered out of him as his muscles strained with the effort to hold back.

Her legs wrapped around his hips, and before he realized what she intended, she dug her heels into his ass and pulled herself onto him until he was buried to the hilt inside her.

A shudder ran down his spine with how good it felt to be deep inside her hot, tight body. But his concern soon took over, and he studied her face for any sign of pain.

She must have seen the worry on his face because she gave him a toothy smile. "I'm fine. More than fine." She wriggled her hips against him. "Now move."

He grinned at her demanding tone. "Yes, little bird."

Setting a measured pace, he started thrusting into her. Sweat pearled on his forehead and down his back as he adjusted his angle until her eyes widened, and she mewled her approval.

Making sure to keep hitting that particular area inside her with every stroke, he moved over her until he was stretched out and supported on his elbows above her body, only leaving enough space between them for her fingers to keep working her clit.

He was quite sure he would have been able to give her an orgasm using his dick alone, but she needed the confidence to take control of her own pleasure when she was with him. And the sooner she realized that he would support anything she needed or wanted in the bedroom, the better.

Her breathing and the flush in her cheeks warned him she was getting close, and he increased his pace. Gritting his teeth to hold off his own release, he pumped his hips to please his mate.

"Gawen, I…" Whatever she had been about to say was cut off by her scream as her channel clamped down on his cock so hard he couldn't move.

His orgasm tore through him when her internal muscles pulsed along his shaft, sending him soaring above the clouds as her body milked him of everything he had to give.

Instinct took over, sharpening and lengthening his teeth. But before he could claim Nes, her teeth sank into his shoulder, sending him spiraling into another orgasm that was even more powerful than the first one. He clamped his jaw over the tender flesh at the crook of her neck, grazing her clavicle, and held on for dear life as the intense pleasure threatened to take his consciousness.

His breathing was ragged when he came back to

reality and his senses started to work again. His mate was breathing heavily close to his ear, and he could feel her chest moving beneath his own.

He was sprawled on top of her, but he wasn't worried about crushing her. She was a shifter and could take his weight without an issue.

Lifting his head, he peeled open his eyes. And almost burst out laughing. Blood was smeared around her mouth and all over her chin, making her look like she had just ripped someone apart with her teeth. Which, on second thought, was sort of what she had done.

"What?" She raised an eyebrow at him in challenge.

"I'm sorry." His laugh escaped, but he managed to tamp it down quickly. "You have...blood on your face. More than a couple of drops too."

Her brows pushed together as she swiped the back of her hand across her mouth. When it came back red with his blood, her gaze immediately snapped to his shoulder.

But he already knew what she would see. His scar might still look pink and new, but a scar was all there was left of her bite. A scar he would cherish until the day he died.

He looked at her shoulder, and his jaw dropped in surprise. Beneath the blood coating her skin, her flesh was healed just like his own.

"Did you always have exceptional healing abilities, or is that something you got from me?" He studied her face, looking for her reaction to his question.

Her brows went up. "Nothing special, no. How does it look?"

His grin grew wide, his chest swelling with pride

and happiness. "Like a mating mark. All healed and beautiful."

She grinned back at him. "That was fast. I like it. Sounds like I can be as reckless as I want from now on since nothing can hurt me."

Growling low in his throat, he got up on his hands and knees while he stared down into her laughing eyes. "Not a chance. I'm not immortal and neither are you. If you try anything like that, I'll tie you up and do wicked things to you."

Her laughter rang out in the room. "That sounds more like an incentive than a caution."

She grabbed his head and pulled him back down to her for a kiss, and he was more than happy to oblige.

It didn't take more than a few swipes of her tongue to get him hot and ready again. And he had a feeling that would be the norm from now on. She was the most perfect creature in the world, after all, and he was the lucky asshole who was her mate.

Breaking their kiss, he rolled onto his back before looking back at her. Her pouting expression made him smile. He clearly wasn't the only one who was ready for a little more action.

"Ride me, my beautiful little bird. Use my body to make yourself come and bring me with you when you go. I want to watch you work up a sweat while I stare at your bouncing breasts."

Her eyes were dark with desire when she slowly rose and climbed on top of him. "I like the way you talk. Keep saying things like that while I sit on your cock, and we have a deal."

He chuckled and got comfortable with his hands folded behind his head. "Fine. I want to feel your pussy strangle my dick when you explode. And make sure to use those talented fingers of yours. Your clit needs to get used to the amount of action it's going to get from now on."

She grabbed his cock and lined it up with her entrance before sinking down on him in one fluid motion until he was buried deep inside her.

"Fuck." His eyes almost rolled back in his head. "Your pussy feels like heaven. If I pass out from sheer pleasure, it will be your fault. I hope you realize that." He was going to have to fight his release every single second until she came.

Nes laughed and rose until just the head of his cock was still inside her. "I guess I just have to find a way to revive you then." Sitting back down, she pinched his nipple.

The combination of pleasure and pain almost had him unloading inside her, and he snarled as he fought for control. *I'm so fucked.*

CHAPTER 47

Nes

Nes felt both sated and pleasantly exhausted by the time they managed to get out of bed in the early evening. The hours since she woke up had opened her eyes to what sex could be like with someone who loved you and encouraged you to find your inner sex goddess.

"Are you ready to join the others?" Gawen smiled down at her. His hair was still dripping from his shower, the droplets running down his hard chest and across his abs until they soaked into the towel hanging low on his hips.

"Perhaps." She couldn't tear her eyes away from the trail of blond hair leading down from his belly button to disappear beneath the towel. Even after hours of continuous sex, the sight was enough to make her want to go back to bed.

"Oh, no-no-no." He put his finger under her chin

and tipped her head back until she was forced to raise her gaze to his. "We need food before we can continue. I won't let you starve just so I can have my wicked way with you. Or you have your wicked way with me, more like it. My balls resemble nuts right now. Small, shriveled walnuts to be precise."

She burst out laughing. "I guess you're right. At least about the food. But perhaps I should have a look at your nuts just to make sure."

He grinned and winked at her. "Nice try, little bird. But I'm afraid you'll have to wait until after we've eaten."

She gave him an exaggerated pout. "You're no fun."

"Yes, I am." His eyes glinted with amusement. "And you've been screaming with the fun we've had for hours. If you had been human, you wouldn't have been able to walk for days. Even as an ordinary wolf, you would have been sore for a while. So you should be grateful you have my healing abilities now."

"I am." She rose on her toes and gave him a quick kiss on his lips. "And that's not the only thing I'm grateful for. I think it's going to take a while for it to sink in that you're truly mine. It feels like I've accidentally wandered into a fairy tale. I mean I've ended up mating a fairy tale creature." She winked at him before turning away to find some clean clothes to wear.

Laughter sounded behind her. "And we're going to live happily ever after."

There was a knock on the door. "Will you two be joining us any time soon?" It was Henry again, and he sounded impatient.

Nes rolled her eyes before she answered. "We'll be there in a few minutes. And I'm still fine. You don't have to worry about me, brother."

"I know." He didn't sound convinced. "But it's been hours, and I'd like to lay eyes on the sister who died on me to see for myself that she's okay."

It wasn't the first time he had come knocking on their door, and perhaps she should have taken pity on him sooner. But she had been otherwise engaged, and he of all people should have understood why.

"As I said we'll be there in a few minutes. So, go on downstairs to your mate and give her a kiss while you're waiting."

Gawen let out a low chuckle, and she grinned at him before bending down to rummage through her bag for some clothes.

***

Gawen

Gawen felt like he was walking around on a cloud of happiness. It was still hard to believe someone like him could get everything he had ever wanted. And he kept having to push away the thoughts that it was too good to be true.

After putting on some fresh clothes, he sat down on the bed to wait for his new mate to get ready. She was fixing her hair in the bathroom with the door open to let him keep an eye on her.

Perhaps he was overreacting, but just the thought of letting her out of his sight for even a minute felt like too much. He wanted to take her hand and never let go again, but that was his own insecurity and fear speaking, and he wouldn't let it rule him ever again.

The three words Nes had said to him before they

mated played in his mind again and made him smile. *You deserve me.* Next to *I love you* those were the three most amazing words he had ever heard.

"I'm ready." Nes came out of the bathroom and headed straight for him. "Are you ready to meet your brother-in-law?" There was a wicked glint in her eyes. "My brother is typically a calm and collected man. But I think he might be ready to hit you by now for keeping me here so long after what happened."

"Keeping you here?" Gawen chuckled as he rose from the bed to smirk down at her. "Then I need to inform him that it was the other way around. Not that I'm complaining."

His eyes strayed to her breasts hidden by her shirt. Even after the countless times they'd had sex, he wanted to rip the clothes from her body and pull her flush against him. Feeling her hot skin against his was the most amazing feeling in the world, and he would always crave it.

"Good. That you're not complaining, that is." She took his hand before pulling him toward the door. "Because otherwise I would have to punish you."

He chuckled as she opened the door, and they walked out into the corridor. "Sounds like I need to make a formal complaint. I have a feeling I might like your form of punishment."

She laughed. "Maybe."

Everyone was gathered in the living room when they arrived, and every head turned in their direction when they stepped into the room.

"About fucking time." Henry was there in an instant, crushing his sister to him in a tight hug.

She chuckled against her brother's chest. "I'm

sorry, but I was kind of busy claiming my mate."

Henry smiled at Gawen over Nes's head. "And I love that for you. For you both. But considering you actually died, it would have been nice to see you awake, if only for a minute."

"I'll remember that next time."

"There won't be a next time!" Gawen and Henry yelled in unison.

Gawen barely held himself back from ripping Nes out of Henry's arms and locking her in a tight embrace. His heart was going a million miles a second at the reminder of her death.

She sighed. "Too soon, huh. I'm sorry."

"It will always be too soon." Gawen sounded angrier than he had intended, but it was the truth. He would never be able to think about what happened without dread and fury filling his guts with acid.

Nes pushed out of Henry's hold on her before turning to Gawen and wrapping her arms around his neck. "It won't happen again. All I want is to be with you. And I'm not about to do anything to jeopardize that."

He bent his head until his forehead was resting against hers. "Please don't joke about it either. The moment I realized you were dead was a thousand times worse than any other moment of my life. You're everything to me, and I can't lose you."

Nes pressed her lips to his. She didn't make any attempt to deepen the kiss, just kept her mouth crushed against his until his heart stopped slamming against his ribs.

He lifted his head and smiled down at her. "I'll have to think of a way to get you back for scaring me like that. You mentioned punishing me earlier, but I—"

"That sounds like something you can discuss later when you're alone." Henry laughed. "I really don't want to know that about my sister."

CHAPTER 48

Aidan

Aidan stood off to the side, studying the various couples in the room. Eight true-mated couples, and they had all found each other during a couple of summer months. It was nothing less than extraordinary, and almost enough to make a man jealous.

He shook his head at his own thought, just managing to stop himself from laughing bitterly at his own stupidity. *I'm not fit to have a mate. I like a casual fuck whenever it suits me, instead of being tied to one woman.*

Except he was sick of it, and the truth was that he hadn't been with a woman for years for that exact reason.

While everyone else was busy talking and laughing, Aidan quietly left the room and went to the kitchen.

The kitchen table was filled with numerous dishes ready to be devoured as part of their celebration to mark the defeat of Amber.

It would also mark his last night with this amazing group of people. He would be leaving early the next morning to go back to his home in London.

But as usual he was unlikely to be staying home for long. Some other vengeful and power-hungry asshole would show up, and he would be required to take care of them. That was his purpose, after all. It was the reason for his existence. To balance good and evil in the world and protect humans from the far more powerful beings existing around them.

He had always been happy, and proud even, to do what needed to be done to maintain order and keep people safe. And he still was. But there was a hollowness in his life that was becoming more prominent every day.

Was that what usually happened when you lived for a really long time? Or was it just him losing his spark as time moved on and nothing really changed?

The world was vastly different compared to a millennia or two ago. And yet both human and supernatural nature had stayed practically the same. People didn't really change.

But he had changed. He had probably experienced everything there was to experience in his lifetime except for one thing. True and endless love. And he was starting to think that love played a more significant role in the world than he had realized.

He had always thought money and power were the main motivations in life and the real drivers of progress, but perhaps they were just substitutes for what people really wanted. Because true love was hard to find. No amount of power or money could create that kind of connection to another person. It had to be found organically, and you had to be ready to grab it when it was there, or the opportunity might be lost forever.

Aidan shook his head at the hopelessness of his situation. Everyone else was allowed to find love if they understood that was what they wanted. Except him. Mating was strictly forbidden for him and his fellow enforcers.

There was no ban on sex as long as it was with another supernatural. Humans were off limits, however, since they were weaker and not supposed to know about the supernatural beings in the world.

Aidan had abided by their rules his entire life. He had been tempted to give in to the lure of a human woman a few times, but not enough to break the rules of their kind.

His phone vibrated in his pocket, and he pulled it out. The number wasn't stored in his phone, but he had it memorized. Lucas was the youngest enforcer, and the one with an affinity for fire.

None of the other enforcers' numbers were registered in Aidan's phone, but if someone happened to get ahold of one of their numbers and check it, they would find them registered to a large phone company.

It was safer that way, considering their targets typically were powerful supernaturals with plenty of money and connections. But the elemental enforcers had money and powerful connections of their own, two of them being Leith and Trevor.

Aidan accepted the call as he walked into the dining room and closed the door behind him. "Lucas. How's it going?"

"Busy." But there was a smile in Lucas's deep voice. "Hunting a rogue vampire in New York who has been praying on women. Unusually difficult to locate, unfortunately. But I'll nail him soon. Markus told me you've been dealing with a particularly nasty creature lately, but that she's been taken care of now. Perhaps you want to join me in America for some vampire hunting? I have a feeling this one is not acting alone."

Aidan ran a hand through his hair, trying to contain a sigh of irritation. He wanted a holiday. Just a few days to focus on something other than the bad guys in the world.

But it wasn't like that was going to happen anytime soon. As soon as they took down one asshole, another one always popped up. "I'll be heading back to London first thing in the morning. If nothing else happens by then that needs my attention, I'll join you in New York."

"Sounds like a plan. Call me tomorrow when you know. Are you all right, Aidan?" Lucas's tone was suddenly filled with concern. "You sound unusually deflated to have just taken down a rogue."

Aidan couldn't contain his irritated sigh this time. "Perhaps I'm getting old, but damn I just want a holiday, you know? Just a few days without anything horrible happening. And preferably far away from a phone."

"I hear you." There was a frown in Lucas's voice. "And I'd like that too. But I won't rest until I've caught this asshole. I've been on his trail for a week, and during that time he's raped at least one woman and killed three. If there's one type of rogue I can't abide by, it's the one that goes after women. I need to catch him, and I need to catch him fast. But as I said, he's unusually good at disappearing, which probably means he has someone meaner and more powerful helping him. And no one backs a rapist other than another rapist."

Aidan nodded, even though Lucas couldn't see him. "True. Which reminds me. The master of the Mateo Brotherhood in Paris is not dead as we had hoped. According to Eleanor, one of his offspring, he's recently started gathering followers again. We'll need to find him before he gets too strong. The longer we wait, the more difficult he will be to take down. And this time we have to make sure we actually kill him. I don't want to face him a third time because we didn't complete the job."

"Fuck." The anger in Lucas's voice was more than warranted. "It's been so long, I had actually forgotten about him and written him off as dead. He tops my list of the vilest creatures I've ever met. I can't believe we have to go after him again. The things he did. I don't even want to think about it."

"I agree." Aidan paced the length of the room. "I'll find out as much as I can about his whereabouts and his current number of followers. And I'll talk to Markus about it. I haven't yet done that. He won't be happy. And neither will Lyn."

"Oh fuck. Lyn." Lucas blew out a breath. "Perhaps it would be better not to tell her until we're ready to go after him. Otherwise, she's likely to hunt him down on her own. I doubt she'll have the patience to wait for us. And although she's one of the best fighters I've ever met, there are limits to how many she can take on at once. The master will kill her, or even worse, capture her and…"

Lucas's voice trailed off, and Aidan knew why. Lyn was one of the master's offspring, just like Eleanor, and after her maker was presumed dead, Lyn had dedicated her life to ridding the world of evil. There was no doubt where her focus would be when she realized that her master was still alive. She had experienced firsthand what that old crusty vampire was capable of, and she would happily risk her own life to stop him.

Aidan stopped in front of one of the windows, staring out at the hills bathed in the golden light from the sun setting. "I'll talk to Markus. But I might have to focus my attention on the master instead of going to New York to help you."

"I don't think there can be any doubt about that, Aidan. I'll dispose of this asshole, and unless there is another urgent situation, I'll come help you."

The sound of people talking and laughing could be heard from the kitchen, and Aidan turned to look at the door. "I have to go. Good luck in New York, Lucas."

"Thank you. Take care, Aidan. We'll talk soon." Lucas disconnected the call.

CHAPTER 49

Nes

Nes walked into the dining room with her plate full of food and her mate right behind her. The enormity of what had happened in the last few days suddenly hit her, and she stumbled and almost dropped her plate.

A strong arm wrapped around her waist and steadied her. "What happened? Are you all right?" Gawen's voice was strained with concern as he carefully guided her toward two seats close to one end of the long table.

Smiling, she turned her head to look up at him. "I'm fine. It just hit me how much has changed in the last few days. My life has changed. *I* have changed. If you'd told me a week ago only a fraction of what would happen, I would have written you off as a complete lunatic. But here I am, with a gorgeous mate and a life I'd never even dreamed of. Not to mention everything I've learned. I thought I knew the world we live in, but apparently I was wrong."

Love filled Gawen's eyes before he leaned in and kissed her forehead. "Let's sit down and eat. Because as soon as we're done, I plan to take you back up to our room and—"

"Not so fast." Aidan chuckled as he passed them on his way to the seat at the end of the table. "You'll have plenty of time for that. Spending a couple of hours with friends and family to celebrate a crucial victory is important. Soon you'll all be heading in different directions, and you never know when you'll be able to see each other again."

Nes shook her head. "Jeez, if that was your celebratory speech, I think you need to lighten up. It came off more doom and gloom than happy and festive."

The enforcer frowned. "I guess I'm not very good at celebrating. To me it usually just means a transition from one problem to the next."

She felt like she should say something encouraging, but she didn't know what to say to someone who literally killed bad guys for a living. It sounded like a hard life and one she couldn't even begin to comprehend. She had no desire to ever experience the dread of the last few days again. But this was Aidan's life every day. Except for the fact that he didn't have a significant other that could be put at risk.

Gawen pulled out her chair, and they sat down next to each other.

"Seeing as we're all present, I want to take this opportunity to say something." Aidan stood with his hands clasped behind his back while his gaze moved from one person to the next around the table. "I've met a lot of courageous people and great warriors in my life, but most of those were people who had chosen that kind of life or at least been trained for it. I have never before met an untrained group of people so determined to save lives even at the risk of losing their own. You're all remarkable."

Aidan's gaze stopped on Gawen. "I have refrained from talking about what happened last night, since I wanted you to be present to fill in the blanks. I'm the one who eventually took Amber's life, but you're the one who made that possible. By keeping her occupied, you allowed me to get close enough to use my magic. Would you please elaborate on what you did to her?"

"Okay." Gawen's voice held a note of strain, and Nes put her hand on his thigh to remind him she was right next to him, safe and sound. "I managed to deflect her magic attacks for a while until she went after Nes. I got distracted by Patrick moving off to the side, and one of her balls of magic hit my mate."

His voice broke, and he cleared his throat before he continued. "After that I acted more on instinct than anything else. I'm a kelpie, and I've got the ability to manipulate water, but never unless I'm in the water or close to it."

"But something changed yesterday." Aidan nodded with a knowing look on his face. "The true range of your abilities have started to unlock, am I right?"

Gawen shrugged. "You say started, but I don't know if there's more to come. Something did change yesterday, though. I managed to hold Amber down and fill her lungs with water, even though I was far from the sea at the time. She was fighting my magic when you arrived and took over. Thank you for showing up when you did. I'm not sure how long I would've been able to hold her, and if she had torn free…"

Aidan nodded. "But your most extraordinary ability, and one I didn't expect, came into play afterward when you brought Nes back from death."

Gawen flinched, and there were more than a few people around the table who sucked in a breath at Aidan's words.

Nes met Henry's intense gaze across the table. His throat was working, and his jaw was tense.

Gawen had told her what had happened, and she had been shocked and amazed at the news. But she hadn't suffered the same emotional trauma at the event as her mate and her brother since she didn't really experience it.

"I don't know the full range of your abilities, Gawen, but there's something more in your ancestry than just kelpie and wolf." Aidan's gaze narrowed. "It might be worth digging into, if only to get an idea of what kind of abilities you can expect to develop over time."

Gawen nodded slowly. "Perhaps."

Aidan crossed his arms loosely over his chest, and his face softened. "And what kind of abilities your children might inherit."

Nes's eyes widened, and she swallowed hard. She wasn't against having children, but since she hadn't intended to mate another shifter, she had always dismissed it as impossible. It would have been awkward to try to explain to a human husband why his kids could change into wolves.

Gawen's hand clasped hers and gave it a squeeze,

and she slowly turned her head to look at him. There was a gentle smile on his face. "Yes, I need to find out before we have children."

Nes was surprised when butterflies took flight in her stomach, and a happy smile threatened to split her face in half.

She would have been more than happy to spend the rest of her life just with Gawen by her side. But perhaps there was more in store for them than she had thought.

But not yet. There were so many things she wanted to experience with her mate before they took that next step.

EPILOGUE

Gawen

Gawen had his hand on his mate's thigh as he let his gaze move from person to person around the long dining table. Most had already finished their breakfast, but there were a few who were still shoveling food into their mouths.

A strange kind of sadness had settled in his chest after they entered the dining room that morning. This would be their last meal together before everyone left to go home. The most horrible and amazing few days of his life were coming to an end.

"What are you thinking about?" The concern in Nes's voice made him turn to her.

Love and gratitude filled his heart and brought a smile to his face. This might be the end of a special time, but it was also the beginning of a bright future with his true mate. "Just that it's sad to know everyone is leaving. I've never met so many amazing people before. It would've been nice to spend more time with everyone now that we don't have to worry about what Amber will do next."

His mate curled her fingers around his hand and squeezed. A soft smile curved her lips. "We'll see them again. Perhaps not everyone at the same time like this, but—"

"Why not?" Jennie gave them a happy smile from across the table before turning to lift an eyebrow at her mate sitting next to her. "We should invite everyone to come and stay for New Years. Or if that's not possible, for a couple of weeks next summer."

Trevor nodded and put an arm around Jennie's shoulders. "Sounds like a plan. Although I think next summer might be the best option. I might have other plans for us for the holidays."

"Really?" Jennie's eyes widened. "What kind of plans?"

Trevor laughed and winked at her. "That's classified."

The blond woman chewed on her bottom lip as she studied her mate's face. "We'll see about that."

"We're in." Duncan grinned from farther down the table. "For the gathering next summer, I mean."

Trevor laughed again. "Considering you live here, I would hope so. What about the rest of you?" His gaze swung around the table. "Do you want to join us next summer for a couple of weeks of fun and adventure? I promise there will be no evil witch to contend with."

"Absolutely," Henry said, smiling at Eleanor.

"Of course." Callum grinned. "It's only fifteen minutes from my house. I mean *our* house." His eyes softened when he looked at Vamika next to him.

"We would be delighted." Leith nodded once, and Sabrina smiled.

"We would love to spend time with all of you again. You can count us in." Fia smiled at Jennie and Trevor, before turning to look at Sabrina and Steph. "But we'll visit at least some of you before then. I need my witch sisters."

"Me too." Steph nodded enthusiastically. "And of course, we'll be here next year. It would be nice to explore these hills when I'm not running for my life. I didn't really get to enjoy it last time."

"Don't remind me." Michael put an arm around her waist and pulled her close. "You could have died up there."

"What about you, Aidan? Would you like to join us next summer?" Trevor turned to the enforcer with his head tilted a little to the side.

Gawen studied the powerful man sitting at the end of the table with his arms crossed over his chest and a neutral expression on his face. He had considered himself the odd one out among these people, but the enforcer was more unique and powerful than he was.

Aidan frowned. "I can't make plans like that I'm afraid. More likely than not, I'll be tracking or fighting some fucker who is trying to destroy other people's lives. But if by some miracle I've got some time off, I'll be happy to join you."

"Well, it's settled then." Jennie's smile was a mile wide, and her eyes were shining with joy. "You're all invited to stay here with us for the first couple of weeks of July next year. I can't wait to see you all again."

Gawen smiled. He couldn't either. An actual

invitation to spend a vacation with friends. It was a first for him, and hopefully the first of many.

∞∞∞

Aidan

Aidan took in the beautiful scenery as he left Fearolc and headed toward Fort William. Who knew when he would be back or even if he would? He couldn't remember the last time he had done something he wanted to do for more than a few hours at a time.

But that was the life of an enforcer. There was never a shortage of evil in the world and people willing to sacrifice others for what they wanted. And it was his job to handle that.

Though, he couldn't help wondering what it would be like to have a significant other to share his life with. Someone who looked at him like the true mates looked at each other.

He let out a sigh so deep he felt it in the pit of his stomach. It couldn't happen. And even if someone happened to look at him like that, he would have to walk away and leave that person behind. Because it was too dangerous to have someone like that in his life. It could destroy him. And short of decapitation, there weren't a lot of other things that could.

"Fuck." He tightened his grip on the steering wheel, trying to force his thoughts over onto something else. Being around all that in-your-face bliss hadn't been a good idea, and he would have to steer clear of that for a while to try to get back to his realistic perspective on life. Longing for something he couldn't have was a distraction he didn't need.

There was one mystery he hadn't been able to solve before he left Fearolc. Who had the ability to use or at least deflect lightning? It was an unusual ability, and not something just anyone could handle. The person would have to be powerful, but none of the most powerful people he had assessed had the ability.

He scratched the stubble on his chin. There was one person who had made him wonder, though, but the magic had been so faint that he had dismissed it as impossible. No one with just a trace of magic would have been able to control an ability like that. Unless the person was also exceptionally good at shielding their magic from detection. So good, in fact, that they didn't even know themselves what they were capable of.

Aidan frowned. It was a mystery for another day. Or perhaps another year. If he was able to join the group the following year, he might be able to conduct a few controlled tests to find out if his suspicions were correct.

Except by going back, he would expose himself to all those true-mated couples again. And two weeks in the middle of all those gooey-eyed individuals wouldn't be good for his mental state.

"I have a nasty vampire to catch." He spoke the words aloud to force his mind onto the topic he should be concerned with.

He had spoken to Eleanor about her maker before he left, but unfortunately, she didn't know where the fucker was at the moment. Apparently he was more than a little paranoid and didn't stay in one place for more than a week. And he never visited the same place twice.

Eleanor's master had been staying right outside London the last time she had spoken to him, but that was months ago. And there was no telling where in the world he was located now.

But Aidan would find him, and he would kill him. Because a sadistic creature like the master would leave too many dead and destroyed humans in his wake.

---THE END---

BOOKS BY CAROLINE S. HILLIARD

Highland Shifters

A Wolf's Unlikely Mate, Book 1
Taken by the Cat, Book 2
Wolf Mate Surprise, Book 3
Seduced by the Monster, Book 4
Tempted by the Wolf, Book 5
Pursued by the Panther, Book 6
True to the Wolf, Book 7
Mated to the Myth, Book 8

Troll Guardians

Captured by the Troll, Book 1
Saving the Troll, Book 2
Book 3 – TBA

Elemental Enforcers

Fire in My Blood, Book 1 – February 2024
Book 2 – TBA

ABOUT THE AUTHOR

Thank you for reading my book. I hope the story gave you an enjoyable little break from everyday life.

I write because I love immersing myself in different worlds where I get to set the rules for what is possible and not. The rules may change from series to series, but there is one rule I will never break. There will always be a HEA (happily ever after) for the couples in my stories.

The characters I create tend to take on a life of their own and push the story in the direction they want, which means my stories don't follow a set structure or specific literary style. But so far, the central theme has been romance, and I don't expect that to change anytime soon.

I hope to spend as much time as possible writing in the years to come. Because the real world is so much better with the added adventure and spice of imagination.

You can find me here:
caroline.s.hilliard@gmail.com
www.carolineshilliard.com
www.facebook.com/Author.CarolineS.Hilliard/
www.amazon.com/author/carolineshilliard/
www.goodreads.com/author/show/22044909.Caroline_S_Hilliard

Printed in Great Britain
by Amazon